THE CASE
OF THE
PHANTOM BULLET

THE CASE
OF THE
PHANTOM BULLET

FROM THE CASE FILES OF
ATTORNEY DANIEL MARCOS

Jeffery Sealing

iUniverse, Inc.
Bloomington

THE CASE OF THE PHANTOM BULLET
From the Case Files of Attorney Daniel Marcos

This is a work of fiction. All of the characters, names, incidents, organizations, and dialogue in this novel are either the products of the author's imagination or are used fictitiously.

iUniverse books may be ordered through booksellers or by contacting:

iUniverse
1663 Liberty Drive
Bloomington, IN 47403
www.iuniverse.com
1-800-Authors (1-800-288-4677)

Because of the dynamic nature of the Internet, any web addresses or links contained in this book may have changed since publication and may no longer be valid. The views expressed in this work are solely those of the author and do not necessarily reflect the views of the publisher, and the publisher hereby disclaims any responsibility for them.

Any people depicted in stock imagery provided by Thinkstock are models, and such images are being used for illustrative purposes only.
Certain stock imagery © Thinkstock.

ISBN: 978-1-4759-5753-2 (sc)
ISBN: 978-1-4759-5754-9 (ebk)

Library of Congress Control Number: 2012919929

Printed in the United States of America

iUniverse rev. date: 10/29/2012

This fictional case is based on Colorado Revised Statutes. Therefore, Colorado Law Procedures, Title 16 and the Criminal Code, Title 18 are mentioned or referenced for legal definitions only. Always consult an attorney in all legal cases. The town named is real but no longer exists. The town, for the purposes of this book, was placed outside of Silverton, Colorado for security reasons due to the September 11, 2001 terrorist attacks. Other towns mentioned are real as they are in the counties so named or mentioned.

To one of my favorite authors in the world Erle Stanley Gardner, you do live on in some of us; Godspeed to you on your journey.

Jeffery Sealing

CHAPTER 1

I t was the first Monday following New Year's Day. The small town of Ironton, Colorado was waking up to the horrible reality that two of its town's people were dead. The town's newspaper, *The Ironton Gazette,* was preparing the early morning edition for delivery. The shootings had managed to garner front-page headlines. In the back of the newspaper, the obituaries, complete with pictures, were published.

According to the front-page article, they had been shot to death by a young Hispanic male that had been arrested, on New Year's Eve, for the shootings. The San Juan County Coroner and Pathologist, Nabiya Quartez, was just completing up the autopsies on the dead bodies.

Nabiya had before her a young Hispanic female about the age of 23 and her young son whom she was breastfeeding when the incident happened. The infant was about eleven months old. She then removed a bullet from the head of the infant. She carefully placed the slug into a metal tray for later analysis. Nabiya was careful to keep detailed notes about the autopsies. She also found a small piece of metal imbedded into the left side ribcage along with some unusual bruising on the right arm of the female.

As Nabiya and her assistant turned the body over, she saw where the bullets had entered. One bullet had entered the left shoulder and sliced through the aorta artery leading out of the heart. There the bullet exited the body just above her left breast, where it entered the infant's skull just above the right eye. The bullet was lodged in the infant's brain, which caused its death. She carefully removed the small metal fragment from the left side ribcage and placed it into the same metal tray as the first bullet. Nabiya removed another, badly damaged bullet from the dead female. She found this bullet had entered the right shoulder and lodged itself in the right lung completely collapsing it.

She completed her notes and took off her gloves. She washed her hands and dried them before signing off on the death certificates, which she put into her "OUT" box. She then put on a fresh pair of gloves and started to pick up the badly damaged bullets and the metal fragment. She put these items into a paper evidence bag, sealed it shut and took off the gloves. She walked outside of the morgue and gave the badly damaged bullets and the unidentified piece of metal to a Colorado Bureau of Investigation agent.

The agent made Nabiya put her signature on the chain-of-custody sheet and her initials went on the seals of the evidence bags. He then took them away. A moment later, the duty Deputy District Attorney Linda Bacara was informed of the autopsy findings. Nabiya entered the morgue and walked into her office. She opened up her Rolodex™, looking for the phone number for the district attorney's office for the 6th Judicial District. She dialed the 24-hour phone number and the duty Assistant District Attorney Linda Bacara answered; it was 0210 hours.

"Duty Assistant District Attorney Linda Bacara speaking," she said.

"Linda, this is Nabiya. I completed the autopsies on those two bodies you brought me."

"All I want to know is was it murder or an accident?"

"In my Pathological opinion, it was murder. The victims were shot more than once which I have seen in cases of premeditated murder and crime of passion killings."

"Thank you, that's all I needed to know right now. I'll be expecting your full autopsy results and your full report in 48 hours. You can release the bodies to the funeral home, now."

"Will do."

Nabiya hung up the phone as her nighttime assistant entered the office.

"Anything else tonight, Nabiya?" he asked.

"Fax off the autopsy reports to Linda Bacara. Her fax number is pre-programmed into the fax machine as number eight."

"Okay."

"Call the funeral home and tell them that the D.A. has released the bodies to them for the funerals. Make sure that they get copies of the death certificates."

"Okay. What about the body transport paperwork?"

"Go ahead and use my stamp here on the right edge of my desk. Make sure to return it when you're done with it and clean up the morgue. Sorry for dragging you out of bed so early in the morning."

"Not a problem, it is one of the privileges of being the on-call coroner."

Nabiya typed up her official report, faxed it off and went home to get some sleep.

Inside of what was nothing more than a double-wide trailer with six jail cells, a young Hispanic male was sitting quietly in cell number two. The Ironton Town Marshal, Jason Beckman, was carefully watching him. The Assistant Town Marshal, Julie Halverston was at her desk, answering the phones and filing paperwork. The Town Marshal, Jason Beckman, was a large hulk of a man. He was muscular, stood six feet ten inches in height and weighed in at two hundred sixty five pounds, with broad shoulders and thick bones. He walked over to Julie's desk.

"Any word from INS?" he asked.

"Just got off the phone with them. The fingerprints we sent them don't match any known illegal aliens that they are looking for," she replied.

"I still think he's an illegal alien. He's just hiding it REAL well."

"I know the feeling."

The phone rang. Julie answered it, handing the receiver to Jason.

"Yes, Linda, what can I do for you?"

"I'm charging him with two counts of First Degree Murder under Colorado Revised Statutes 18-3-102. One count under section 1, subparagraph D and one count under section 1, subparagraph F. Does he have legal counsel and did you read him his Miranda Rights?"

"No, he doesn't have legal counsel yet, but yes, I did read him his Miranda Rights in both English and Spanish."

"Good and I assume that you documented such in the arrest report?"

"Yes ma'am."

"He has to appear before a judge in accordance with Colorado Revised Statutes 16-7-201 within 72 hours."

"72 hours sounds about right, Linda. Do you know who the judge could be?"

"The Honorable Larry Bishop I think."

"Good, tough judge, especially on illegal aliens who commit major crimes in his judicial district," said Marshal Beckman as he looked at the young man.

The young man moved uneasily on the bunk in his cell.

"By the way, do you have any criminal defense lawyers up there or any public defenders in the town?"

"Yes, Attorney Daniel Marcos, Esquire. He just set up shop, before Christmas, on the edge of town."

"Oh, this is going to be fun with one of my former law school students, especially when he finds out who the prosecutor is going to be in the case."

"Do you think Judge Bishop will move this man to the San Juan County Sheriff's office in Silverton?"

"Maybe, or maybe not. If the San Juan County Sheriff's department shows up, turn the prisoner over to them."

"Yes ma'am."

"Did you allow him to make his phone call?"

"Yes ma'am, he called a relative."

"Well, I'll see if Judge Bishop will allow an extension on the arraignment until the defendant has consulted legal counsel."

"I'll be expecting your phone call."

"Good-bye."

Linda called Judge Bishop and explained the situation. The judge agreed to the extension of time for the arraignment until counsel for the accused could be acquired. The judge heard from Linda that perhaps Attorney Daniel Marcos, a known rival of the judge and prosecutor, might be the young man's legal counsel.

Daniel Marcos walked into his office that same Monday morning. It was warm in the office, despite the sub-zero temperatures outside. There was no new snow, but what little there was, was piled up almost waist deep at the entrance to his office. He closed the door and turned to his secretary, Lynn Lyons. He saw she was reading the *Ironton Gazette's* front-page article. She handed the newspaper to Daniel. He briefly read over the article and handed it back to her as he took off his heavy coat.

He poured himself a cup of coffee and walked into his inner office. He started checking his phone messages. When he had listened to the last message, he had finished off his cup of coffee and went about unpacking the last box of law books. When he had put the last law book on the bookshelf, he sat down at his desk. He reread the article completely; this time he noted that the district attorney's office of the 6ᵗʰ Judicial District was going to file formal charges soon. He also saw that Linda Bacara was being given the first prosecuting attorney rights.

He put the newspaper back down as the outer door to his law office opened. He looked up and saw an older looking, Hispanic gentleman come inside. He went to Lynn's desk and started talking to her. She said something to him and he sat down in the waiting room. Lynn came into Daniel's office and whispered something into his right ear. Daniel stood up and walked out into the waiting area.

"Why don't you come in and talk to me?" asked Daniel as he pointed to his inner office and shaking the man's right hand.

"Thank you, sir," said the man with a heavy Spanish accent as he followed Daniel into his office where the man closed the door. The man took off his straw hat and hung it up on the hat rack, which was just to the right of the door.

The gentleman took off his heavy coat, setting it down in the chair to Daniel's left. He then sat down in the chair directly in front of Daniel. Daniel could see that the man's eyes were red from crying. The man then used his right index finger to tap the newspaper headline.

"My brother was arrested for these murders, but he didn't do it. I was with him, sir," he said as he choked on tears.

"I see. How did you get my name and address?" asked Daniel suspiciously.

"From the district attorney's office in Silverton. A nice lady by the name of Linda Bacara was so helpful."

"Okay. You know that if a jury convicts your brother of these murders, he faces life in prison without parole."

"Yes, the district attorney explained that to me and my brother. That is why I have come here to hire your services. My family is originally from Honduras, but my grandfather, grandmother, father, etc., are all U.S. citizens and we have money; how much?" he asked as he withdrew his wallet.

"$485.00 an hour; minimum ten hour retainer. I will then bill you after the money has been used up."

"Will this be enough?" asked the man as he dropped three, $5,000 bills on the desktop.

"Well, sir, it appears that you have hired my services," said Daniel as he looked at the bills. The bills were 1961 series.

"Thank you, sir. I know you will do your best."

"Please see my secretary outside for a receipt. Let her know where you are staying as well as a phone number that I can call you or my client at anytime of the day or night."

"Yes, sir."

"What's your name?"

"Roberto Rivera III."

After the man left, Daniel stepped outside to see Lynn.

"Find out when the arraignment is as well as who the prosecutor and judge are."

"Right away. Do you think we will need Kim?" she asked as she started dialing phone numbers.

"Yes, get her up here as soon as possible."

Lynn spent the next hour and half on the phone. When she had finished off the last phone call, she took her notepad with the notes she had taken into Daniel's office. She entered the office.

"What do you have on my client?" asked Daniel.

"He's being held at the Ironton jail by your friend, Marshal Beckman."

"That's great. What else?" he asked as he rolled his eyes.

Daniel and the town marshal weren't exactly the best of friends. Daniel, in his younger days, had caused much mischief and problems for then newly appointed town marshal of Ironton. The marshal never thought very highly of Daniel. In fact, Daniel made the entire town promise not to say anything to the marshal about him going to law school.

"File a Writ of Habeas Corpus. I would like to see my client at the earliest opportunity," said Daniel.

"Will do. I found out that the judge is Larry Bishop and the prosecutor is Assistant District Attorney Linda Bacara."

"Two more nails in the defense's coffin," muttered Daniel.

"I suppose so. If you don't have anything else, I'll get started on the writ."

"Prepare Discovery Motions, please. I would like to see the evidence against my client."

"All ready done," she said holding a stack of paperwork ready to be signed by either a judge or one of the district attorneys.

"Well, get all that paperwork signed by Judge Bishop."

"Right away."

She left the office and returned about forty-five minutes later. Judge Bishop had signed all of the paperwork. Daniel looked up at her because she was shaking slightly.

"Something wrong, Lynn?" asked Daniel taking the paperwork from her. As he singled out the writ to see his client, he grabbed his heavy jacket.

"I believe that Judge Bishop tried to intimidate and interrogate me while I was in his chambers about this case."

"What did you tell him?"

"Nothing. I told him, 'No comment.'"

"Good girl."

Daniel departed the office. He walked through dry snow about mid-calf deep. Daniel reached down and picked up some of the dry snow and tried to make a snowball. The dry snow simply vanished in his warm hands leaving only a small amount of water behind. He continued walking towards the double-wide trailer that served as the police station. He opened the door just as Marshal Julie Halverston was leaving. She merely stared at Daniel and smiled as she stepped into the police vehicle, driving off.

"Well, come on in, Mr. Marcos Esquire," said a deep voice.

"I'm here to see my client, sir," said Daniel, handing Jason the writ as he stood up, bumping his head on the low ceiling. Jason took the paperwork.

"Right this way, counselor."

Jason said some commands in Spanish to Daniel's client. The young man stood up and turned around in his cell. He put his hands together behind his back and turned around in his cell. He put his hands out through the extra wide slot in the bars.

Jason handcuffed the man before he opened the cell door. Jason escorted the young man out of the cell to a chair that was in front of Daniel. Jason closed the cell door. The marshal then stepped outside of the trailer, locking the door. The young man shifted a little in the chair. He looked up at Daniel.

"Are you my attorney or public defender?" asked the young man with a light Spanish accent.

"I am your attorney. Your brother hired my services this morning; sorry it took so long for me to get here."

"It's okay. They're treating me okay and I haven't told them anything yet."

"Good. What's your name?" asked Daniel, pulling out a small tape recorder from his left, jacket pocket, pressing the RECORD button as he set it down on the desktop.

"Juan Rivera, sir."

"Where and when were you born?"

"Nogales Arizona, October 18th, 1992 at 3:18 pm in St. Judith's Hospital on Valirez Street."

"Am I to assume that you're a U.S. Citizen, then?"

"Yes. Since my parents were illegal aliens, in the beginning, I took courses in English and took the U.S. Citizenship test in October of 2010. I became a U.S. Citizen about 3 weeks ago."

"What happened to your parents?"

"They were deported when INS raided the meat packing plant where they were working. My brother took me into his house and has raised me since I was 15."

"Do you still have family in Honduras?"

"Yes. But, I haven't seen my parents or other relatives since they were deported."

"Have you had any contact with your family in Honduras? Any letters, emails, faxes, telegrams etc.?"

"No. Just what my brother tells me."

"I'll try and get you in front of Judge Bishop as soon as possible. If I can get bail arranged for you, don't run away. It will look bad for you and your case."

"I understand, sir."

"Please be advised that until I can prove your citizenship status, you might be considered a flight risk. The judge may deny you bail or he may order you to a more secure facility in either Telluride or Durango."

"I understand, sir."

"Were you read your rights?"

"Yes, sir, in both English and Spanish."

"All right, then I won't have to read your rights to you again. Were you allowed to make a phone call?"

"Yes, I was also allowed to make my one phone call."

"Where are your citizenship papers located?"

"My citizenship papers are in the safe at my brother's place and I have the key to the drawer where the papers are located."

"That's good. Where's that key now?"

"In my personal effects that are locked up next to me," said Juan, using his eyes to point to the large safe that was to his left.

"I want you to relax. Don't say anything to anyone without my say so, unless the questions are about you personally such as name, date of birth, etc."

"Yes, sir."

"Do you need anything?" asked Daniel, pushing the STOP button and putting the tape recorder back into the same pocket.

"No, sir."

"Have you talked to the District Attorney yet?"

"Yes, this morning and I told her that I wouldn't say anything to her without my attorney present."

"Good job. We will have to make a statement to the DA sooner or later; good-bye."

Daniel left the trailer and returned to the office. Upon arrival, he found reporters hanging all around the office entrance. They were asking him all sorts of questions. He ignored them and made it inside to his inner office. Jessica Kim was there along with Lynn. He took off his heavy jacket and handed the tape recorder to Lynn. She disappeared into the outer office, locking the door to the outside. She put on her headphones and started typing as the tape recorder played. The phone on Daniel's desk started ringing.

"Hello?" asked Daniel.

"This is Judge Bishop, is Attorney Daniel Marcos, Esquire there?" he asked.

"Speaking," said Daniel.

"Arraignment will be in my courtroom D at 2:30 pm tomorrow."

"Very well."

"Good-bye."

Daniel hung up the phone and turned to face Jessica when the phone rang a second time.

"Hello?"

"When can I expect a statement from your client?" asked Linda harshly.

"Tomorrow morning at 10:15 am in the Ironton Town Marshal's office."

"I'll see you and your client tomorrow then."

"Good-bye."

He hung up the phone and turned back to Jessica.

"Please inform my client about the deposition with the DA in the morning. Try and get some background from my client on his family history. Have Lynn call ahead so that my client will speak to you."

"I'll be back."

She left and Daniel started writing down notes on a notepad. Lynn brought in the transcribed notes. He reviewed them and then looked up at her.

"Lynn, call Marshal Beckman and have him come to my office."

"Right away," she said.

Forty-five minutes later, Marshal Beckman entered the outer office. Daniel looked up and motioned for him to come into his inner office. Marshal Beckman entered Daniel's office and closed the door.

"What can I do for you, counselor?" he asked, smiling.

"I need a seizure warrant issued for something in my client's personal property which you have locked up," said Daniel.

"I'm going to regret this, but what in your client's personal property do you need?"

"A small key. The key may be silver, gold or other color."

"Why not just ask your client for the key?"

"Without a seizure warrant, taking that key from his personal property that is under your control would violate his 4th Amendment right to unreasonable search and seizure. I don't want any contamination of the evidence that I obtain for my client with this key."

"Type up the affidavit and I'll get the warrant; fair enough, counselor?"

"Fair enough. However, I need a search warrant as well."

"I'm not even going to ask what you need the search warrant for. Just type up the affidavit and I'll get the search warrant."

"Thank you, sir."

"Anything else, counselor? Since I am about to get off work here, shortly, will it be okay for Marshal Halverston to serve the warrants?"

"Marshal Halverston will do fine, sir. I would like those warrants served tonight. Do you know who the duty judge might be?"

"His Honor, Judge Kyle Tillman, I believe."

"Good, if you can get him to sign those warrants tonight, I would appreciate it. Would it be alright if my private investigator went along with Marshal Halverston to serve the warrants?"

"Not a problem, I'll let her know."

"Thank you, Marshal Beckman. I will have those affidavits typed up, notarized and delivered to your office in the next thirty minutes, okay?"

"Sounds okay to me," he said as he stood up and walked out of Daniel's office.

Daniel dictated the affidavits to Lynn. She typed them up and Daniel reviewed them before making some minor changes. When the final drafts were completed, Daniel and Lynn went to the Ironton National Bank. There, they saw the bank notary, Mrs. Ethel Stockton. She notarized the affidavits when Daniel had signed them. Lynn delivered the affidavits to Marshal Halverston. Marshal Halverston took the affidavits over to the courthouse and was able to get the warrants issued. His Honor, Judge Kyle Tillman, signed the warrants, but was a little perplexed by Daniel's reasoning at first. It wasn't until later that night that he understood Daniels' reasoning for the warrants.

Jessica had returned to the office and was waiting for Lynn and Daniel to return. Jessica had notes that she handed to Daniel. Daniel took the notes and set them down on his desktop.

"Did you tell my client about his appointments?" asked Daniel.

"Yes, I did."

"Good. Get back over to the marshal's office; you will be riding along with Marshal Halverston when she serves the warrants."

"Okay."

"I'll review your notes in the morning; good-night."

"Good-night, Daniel."

Daniel called Roberto and told him that the Assistant Town Marshal, Julie Halverston and his private investigator were heading out to his property with search and seizure warrants. Daniel asked that Roberto cooperate fully with Marshal Halverston and Jessica in the gathering of the items requested on the warrants. Lynn returned and shutdown her computer and started the long drive home to Telluride from Ironton. Daniel locked up the notes in the office safe. He stuck around in his inner office until Kim returned. Daniel locked up the paperwork in the office safe and went home; tomorrow was going to be a very long day for him and his client.

CHAPTER 2

Daniel was in the office early the next morning. He poured himself a cup of coffee and started reviewing his client's family history. When Lynn came in, Daniel had her scan the copy of the Citizenship Certificate and other papers into the computer. Lynn printed out a copy of the Citizenship Certificate. Daniel noticed who the judge was that had signed it. He handed the copy back to Lynn.

"Fax that copy over to Linda at the DA's office," said Daniel.

"Okay; anything else?"

"Get that judge's phone number and ask Her Honor to stand-by the phone after 2:30 pm today, just in case."

"Will do."

"Also, make sure that the original gets back into Roberto's safe."

"Okay."

Jessica entered the office. Daniel saw her and motioned for her to enter his inner office.

"Great work last night. I'll be getting the list of witnesses soon. I want you to go talk to them."

"Will do. Anything else while I am here?"

"Get your range-finding equipment ready as well as your video camera."

"Okay," she said, writing the things down Daniel had said.

The phone rang. Lynn put the call through to Daniel; it was Linda. He picked up the phone as Jessica was leaving.

"Greetings, counselor, what can I do for you?" asked Daniel.

"Thought you might want to discuss a plea bargain."

"A plea bargain, eh and before the arraignment? What are you willing to offer my client?" asked Daniel, already suspicious of her intentions.

"Second Degree Murder, 18-3-103, Section 3, Subparagraph B; 18 years."

"No dice, you have yet to prove a crime of passion was involved. I will offer Manslaughter, 18-3-104, Section 1, Subparagraph A; 10 years."

"No can do. How about Criminally Negligent Homicide, 18-3-105; 2 years?"

"Maybe. I will counter offer with Disorderly Conduct, 18-9-106, Section 1, Subparagraph E, fine only, no jail time?"

"No way."

"I'll see you in court, then, counselor," said Daniel, hanging up the phone.

Daniel put on his heavy jacket and left the office. He went to the marshal's office to be with his client. Then Linda arrived to get Juan's statement. Juan answered all of her questions with simple yes and no answers without elaborating on anything. When the last question had been answered, Juan was taken back to his cell. Daniel walked outside with Linda, who spoke first.

"I'm still going to charge your client with two counts of First Degree Murder 18-3-102. I'll be willing to spare the taxpayers a lot of time and money if your client pleads guilty to both charges."

"In exchange for what?"

"Life in prison without parole."

"No way, counselor. You would have to prove premeditation, pre-planning and intent."

"I believe I just proved all of those when I asked your client if he and the deceased knew each other intimately."

"So, they were probably high school sweethearts or something like that; who cares."

"Really? Or, is it that the child was his and he killed both of them to stop that fact from being found out?"

"Valid point, counselor. I will see you at the arraignment."

"Good day, counselor."

Daniel walked back inside to speak to Juan. The marshal stepped outside to give them some privacy.

"Juan, I will be with you in Courtroom D today at 2:30 pm, when you are formally charged."

"Thank you. I know that my brother has hired a good man; will I get bail?"

"Not yet. The preliminary hearing is where I will ask for reasonable bail. Be prepared that it may not happen. I have a feeling that the DA and the judge will label you as a flight risk."

"I am an American citizen; where would I go?"

"Back to Honduras, which has no extradition treaty with the U.S. if the person faces a death sentence for the crime committed."

"Oh, I see now."

"When was the last time you saw your mother and father?"

"August 18th, 2001, before the INS raided the meat packing plant. Of course, since I was born on U.S. soil, the INS judge said I could stay in the U.S., but my parents had to go because they were here illegally."

"So, you've had no direct or indirect contact with your parents for over 10 years, then? I hate to keep asking this same question, but it is one way to see if my client is lying to me."

"Yes. When I graduated from Silverton High School, my brother videotaped the ceremony. Afterwards, he mailed it to an uncle in Honduras. The uncle was supposed to give the videotape to my parents."

"Okay. When, or if, I can get bail arranged, you need to come talk to me."

"I will, sir."

"I have some paperwork to do, so I have to go."

Juan was once again escorted back to his cell. Daniel returned to his office to try and dictate some memos. Once again, he had to get past the throng of reporters asking questions to get into his outer office. At 2:15 pm, Daniel walked out of his office, through the reporters and down the street to the Ironton Courthouse. He entered courtroom D and waited for the judge to enter. Judge Bishop entered the courtroom as the bailiff, Sergio Martinez, asked everyone to rise.

"All rise. Courtroom D in the 6th Judicial District, San Juan County, in the town of Ironton, Colorado, is now in session. The Honorable Judge Larry Bishop, presiding," he said.

"Be seated, this courtroom will now come to order," said Larry.

Larry opened up the court docket with the case number of 11CR1, *The People V. Juan Rivera*. He looked over the arrest report, DA complaint filing and the accused's prior arrest record; nothing was on Juan's criminal background check. He looked over a supplemental report from the Department of Justice from INS; *INS V. Alethia and Juarez Rivera,* case number 01-1125, 9th Federal Circuit Court for Nogales, Arizona. He looked over some other stuff in the file and looked at the defendant. Judge Bishop put on his glasses and saw that the accused had legal counsel present. He also noted that the DA was present as well.

"Will the defendant please rise," said Larry.

Juan stood up with Daniel; Linda stood up as well. Lynn entered the courtroom and tapped Daniel on his right shoulder. He turned around and Lynn handed him a piece of paper. The paper contained the phone number for the judge who had signed Juan's Citizenship Certificate

"In the case of *The People V. Juan Rivera,* case number 11CR1, the defendant has been advised of his rights in both English and Spanish. This is evidenced to this court by the defendant's signature on the Miranda Rights affidavit. For the court's records, Mr. Rivera, were you advised of your rights?" asked Larry.

"Yes, Your Honor, I have been advised of my rights in both English and Spanish," replied Juan.

"So noted. Bailiff, please hand the defendant this statement," said Larry, handing the bailiff some paperwork.

The bailiff handed Juan the paperwork.

"I ask you now, Mr. Rivera, is that your signature on those forms?" asked Larry.

Juan looked through the forms.

"Yes, Your Honor, that is my signature on each of those forms," replied Juan.

"So noted," said Larry who was busy signing some paperwork on his bench.

The bailiff took the paperwork and handed it back to Larry. The judge put the paperwork back into the file. He looked at the defendant once again.

"Mr. Rivera, this court, due to recent changes in the arraignment law, Colorado Revised Statutes 16-7-201, has to ask you if you can read, speak and write English?" asked Larry.

"Yes, Your Honor, I can read, speak and write English as well as Spanish and I can speak German."

"So noted. Mr. Rivera, are you a U.S. Citizen and/or are you or your parents/legal guardians here illegally?"

"I am a U.S. Citizen by birth plus I have taken and passed the U.S. Citizenship exam in addition to being sworn in as a U.S. Citizen on December 29th of 2010."

"Were your parents U.S. Citizens or where they here illegally?"

"Objection Your Honor, irrelevant and immaterial," said Daniel.

"Objection overruled. The accused will answer the question," said Larry coldly.

"My parents were here illegally in the United States and were deported after the INS raided the meat packing plant they were working at. My brother, Roberto Rivera III, has raised me since I was 15, Your Honor."

"Where were you born?"

"Nogales, Arizona."

"Your Honor, I have an official copy of his birth certificate," said Linda.

"Defense counsel?"

"Your Honor, my esteemed colleague should also have a copy of my client's citizenship certificate and other citizenship paperwork. Even though my client does not need either one."

"Do you wish to say anything else, Mr. Marcos?" asked Larry, loudly.

"Yes, Your Honor. Furthermore, Her Honor Judge Krysta Johnson of the 10th Federal Circuit Court signed the serial numbered Citizenship Certificate and other paperwork. I have her phone number."

"Why do I need Her Honor's phone number?" asked Larry.

"If you please, Her Honor has been advised to be available and to be expecting your phone call," said Daniel, handing the bailiff the piece of paper with the phone number on it.

The bailiff took the phone number and the copies of the paperwork to the judge. The judge looked at Linda.

"District Attorney Bacara, do you have any objections to the phone call or the paperwork?" asked Larry.

"No objections, Your Honor," she replied, smiling.

The judge dialed the number he had been given. The phone rang a few times before a woman answered. Judge Bishop put the call on speakerphone so that everyone could hear the conversation.

"Hello?" asked Krysta.

"This is Judge Larry Bishop in Courtroom D, in Ironton, Colorado. I am located in a Courthouse within the 6th Judicial District of Colorado, located in San Juan County. Is this Her Honor Krysta Johnson, 10th Federal Circuit Court Judge?" asked Larry.

"Yes, it is, Your Honor Judge Bishop. I was informed by Attorney Daniel Marcos Esquire to be in my chambers in the event you called about one Juan Rivera."

"Then I will make my question to the point. On the 29th of December of 2010, did you swear in, as a U.S. Citizen, one Juan Rivera?" asked Larry.

"Yes, I did. His U.S. Citizenship Certificate Serial Number should be, according to my court records, 235057512. I remember him well, Your Honor."

"Will you please tell this court why you remember Mr. Rivera so well."

"He felt that, although he was born on U.S. soil, which makes him a U.S. Citizen, his parents were here in the U.S. working illegally at a meat packing plant. I tried to get the details on his parents deportation case, but couldn't. That made me a little suspicious."

"I can understand that, Your Honor. Please continue."

"He wanted to make sure that if someone called into question his loyalties or citizenship, he could prove to them he was really a U.S. Citizen and that his loyalty was to the United States of America."

"Thank you, Your Honor, so noted; good-bye," said Larry hanging up the phone.

Daniel leaned over and whispered into Juan's right ear.

"You have dual citizenship, then, because of your parents, don't you?"

"Yes, sir."

"Do you have a passport?" asked Daniel.

"No, I do not, sir. I applied for one on December 30th 2010, but I won't know until March of this year if I got it or not."

"Thank you."

The judge looked back at Juan.

"In the case of *The People V. Juan Rivera,* case number 11CR1. Mr. Rivera, having been advised of your Constitutional rights under both the federal and state constitutions, the charges against you are: 2

counts of First Degree Murder under Colorado Revised Statutes, Title 18, Article 3, Part 102. One Count of violating Subparagraph D and one count of violating Subparagraph F; how do you plead?"

"Not guilty, Your Honor," said Daniel.

"So noted; a plead of not guilty has been entered by Mr. Rivera's defense attorney, Daniel Marcos Esquire. The charges are: 2 counts of Second Degree Murder, under Colorado Revised Statutes, Title 18, Article 3, Part 103 Section 2; how do you plead?"

"Not guilty, Your Honor," said Daniel.

"So noted; a plead of not guilty has been entered by Mr. Rivera's defense attorney, Daniel Marcos Esquire. The charges are: 2 counts of Manslaughter, under Colorado Revised Statutes, Title 18, Article 3, Part 104 Section 1, Subparagraph A; how do you plead?"

"Not guilty, Your Honor," said Daniel.

"So noted; a plead of not guilty has been entered by Mr. Rivera's defense attorney, Daniel Marcos Esquire. This concludes the arraignment hearing. The preliminary hearing is set for Friday, January 7th, in this same courtroom, at 8:00 am. The defendant, for the time being, is remanded to the custody and care of the Ironton Town Marshal, Marshal Jason Beckman."

Judge Bishop was silent for a few seconds before looking directly at the prosecutor.

"What charge or charges are The People going to pursue?"

"All of them, Your Honor."

"So noted," said Larry as he banged his gavel down.

"All rise," said the bailiff as Judge Bishop left the courtroom.

Everyone left the courtroom. Daniel returned to his office. This time he entered the office without seeing any reporters at all. When he entered the outer office, Lynn handed Daniel some paperwork and the day's mail. Daniel continued walking into his inner office. He sat down at his desk, opened and read the daily mail. He then read the paperwork that Lynn had handed him.

The paperwork consisted of an affidavit, typed up by Lynn and notarized by the Ironton City Attorney's Clerk. This was attached to a temporary restraining order. Daniel smiled as he read that the restraining order was issued to the reporters ordering them to maintain a 25-yard perimeter from the office. He put the paperwork down as Lynn stepped around the corner.

"Nice touch for those reporters; thank you, Lynn," said Daniel.

"Thank you, Daniel. Those reporters were getting on my nerves. Jessica is ready to go whenever you are," said Lynn.

"Tell her, Saturday morning, the 8th of January. The preliminary hearing is set for the morning of the 7th of January."

"I'll let her know."

"Send those Discovery Motions over to the DA's office that I dictated to you earlier. Ask the DA if it is possible to tour the crime scene and the scene where the town marshal arrested my client."

"Will do. By the way, Roberto is here."

"He was in the courtroom today during the arraignment. Send him in."

Roberto entered the office.

"I have a feeling that the judge and the DA don't like my brother very much," said Roberto.

"You're right, they don't. However, it is not just your brother, it is most people from outside the U.S. They perceive them as being here illegally and trying to pull a fast one on the criminal justice system."

"I see. Can you do anything about this issue?"

"I plan on asking for a Change of Venue because I don't think your brother can get a fair trial here in Ironton."

"Where would the trial be held, then?"

"If the Change of Venue is granted, the trial could be held in either Durango or Grand Junction."

"You're a good man, sir. Here, Juan's parents gave me this to give to you for your hard work," said Roberto, handing Daniel a $10,000.00 bill.

"See my secretary for a receipt," said Daniel as he took the money. The bill was a 1954 series.

"Thank you, sir and I had always been told that lawyers, in the U.S. anyway, were not nice people."

"There are only a few in this world that are not nice, Roberto; good-night."

"Good-night to you, too, sir."

Roberto left the office. Daniel locked up the money in the office safe before going home.

CHAPTER 3

The date for the preliminary hearing had arrived. Daniel had already filed the Discovery Motions. He obtained a list of the witnesses from the DA's office the day before. He gave the list to Jessica Kim for her to interview the witnesses for the defense. Daniel entered the courtroom just as Marshal Beckman brought in Juan in handcuffs. Jason put Juan in the seat next to Daniel. Daniel also saw that Juan was in an orange "jump" suit. The bailiff stood up as Judge Bishop entered the courtroom.

"All rise, Courtroom D is now in session. The Honorable Judge Larry Bishop, presiding," said Sergio.

Larry put on his glasses, opened up the case file and sat down in his chair at the bench. He then picked up his gavel and banged it down on the desktop.

"Be seated. This is the preliminary hearing in the case of *The People V. Juan Rivera*, case number 11CR1. The defendant has been advised of his rights once again in both English and Spanish. Does the defendant wish to request for bail?"

Daniel stood up.

"Yes, Your Honor. My client asks that this court set a reasonable amount for bail."

"So noted. Does the prosecution have anything to say about the defendant's bail request?"

"The prosecution, representing The People, request that bail be denied on the basis of the charges being capital offenses and that the defendant is a flight risk," said Linda smiling.

"Objection, Your Honor. Although my client could flee to another geographical location, in this case, Honduras, he has neither the connections nor the desire to go there. Unless my client doesn't like the snow and cold of Colorado in January."

The courtroom spectators and Roberto all chuckled at the statement before Larry banged his gavel down.

"Silence in my courtroom!" yelled Larry.

Daniel continued despite the laughter.

"Honduras does have an extradition treaty with the U.S. provided that the criminal does not face a death sentence for the crime or crimes he or she has committed. This extradition treaty is current according to the U.S. State Department."

Daniel could tell a sparring match was about to erupt between him and Linda.

"Objection, Your Honor. The People don't have the money to return the defendant to this court."

"Your Honor, I will be happy to pay for the extradition, should it become necessary, to assist The People. If my client should decide to flee this court's jurisdiction."

"The People will stipulate to defense counsel's terms if extradition becomes necessary."

"Objection sustained. Does the prosecution have evidence to show that the defendant is such a flight risk?" asked Larry.

"The People have evidence that the defendant has a passport and could easily flee."

"Objection, Your Honor. My client has applied for a passport from the Seattle, Washington, passport office, but has not received it. If The People have possession of my client's passport, I respectfully request that both the passport and the seizure warrant used to obtain said passport be delivered into evidence."

"Objection overruled. The People should show the evidence to defense counsel in accordance with the 4th, 6th and 14th Amendments."

"All The People have, Your Honor, is the letter from the Seattle, Washington, passport office stating that the defendant has a passport."

"Was the passport mailed to the defendant?" asked Larry.

"Yes, Your Honor, the passport was mailed to the defendant's listed address, on his passport application, on the 5th of this month," replied Linda.

"Your Honor, if my client receives his passport at his listed address, which was, according to the post office, not to happen until March of this year, my client will voluntarily surrender said passport to the DA's office."

"Will that be satisfactory to The People?" asked Larry.

"The People will stipulate to the terms," said Linda.

"Your Honor, my client would like to make sure that he gets his passport and other personal items back, at the end of this trial. I respectfully request that the DA's office serve my client with a seizure warrant for said passport."

"Do The People have any objections to defense counsel's request, Linda?"

"The People have no objections, Your Honor."

"So noted."

"Your Honor, my client's 8th Amendment rights are clearly being violated at this time."

"On what grounds, counselor?"

"My client is dressed in this orange 'jump' suit that says 'PROPERTY OF THE IRONTON TOWN MARSHAL'S OFFICE' on the back of it and the handcuffs."

"This is a preliminary hearing, not a trial."

"Your Honor, potential jurors can see my client dressed like this," Daniel said, pointing to Juan, "and prejudge him to be guilty."

"So noted. This court will allow the defendant to wear appropriate courtroom attire. Is that okay, counselor?" asked Larry.

"I agree, Your Honor, as long as The People have no objections," said Daniel, looking over at Linda.

"The People have no objections, Your Honor," she replied, smiling.

"Now, about bail. How much money does your client have on him right now?" asked Larry.

"$500.00, Your Honor," said Daniel, smiling, as he knew he had the $500.00 in his wallet.

"So noted. Since The People couldn't provide enough evidence to prove that the defendant is indeed a flight risk, bail will be set at $50,000.00," said Larry, banging his gavel down.

"Thank you, Your Honor," said Daniel.

"This court is adjourned. The trial will be set for the 2nd of February of this year in my courtroom at 9:00 am. Bailiff, please remove the defendant and remand him back into the custody of the Ironton Town Marshal, Jason Beckman."

Sergio stood up and took Juan away to one of the many holding cells that were part of the backside of the courthouse. As Daniel got ready to leave the courtroom, he stopped Linda.

"I would like to tour the crime scene, but as of yet, I haven't received permission," said Daniel.

"Sure, I'll let you tour the crime scene and the arrest scene as you requested. Assistant Town Marshal Julie Halverston will escort you and your private investigator at all times; is that okay?"

"Thank you."

Daniel left the courtroom and arrived back at the office. He found no reporters anywhere on the property or the street. He entered the office and Lynn handed him his phone messages. He saw the one message from Roberto. As he poured himself a cup of coffee, he called Roberto first.

"Hello?" asked Roberto.

"Roberto, this is Daniel, you called me?"

"Daniel. $50,000.00 is a lot of bail money."

"Relax, you only have to pay 20% of it to the bail bondsman."

"Oh, that is good news. How much is 20%?"

"$10,000.00, but you had better hurry to the bail bondsman's office. It is in Telluride and with current road conditions it might take you two to two and half hours to get there and back."

"What's the bail bondsman's name?"

"It's a company called A and A Bail Bonds."

"Address?"

"25051 West Highway 550."

"Okay."

"Anything else?"

"No."

Daniel hung up the phone and went about his normal business. Daniel saw that Mr. Peabody had called him about the Keller place up Smith Canyon Road. Daniel read over the rest of the messages and called Mr. Peabody.

"Mr. Peabody, this is Attorney Daniel Marcos Esquire; you called?"

"Yes, sir. I am willing to now counter-offer with $125,000.00 more than the previous offer along with an extra $150,000.00 for the water, mineral and other rights to the property. I would also like to sweeten the deal further for you to the tune of $120,000.00 in lawyer's fees," said Mr. Peabody.

"Very well, Mr. Peabody. I will call Mr. Keller right now and inform him of your increased counter-offer. Can I call you back at this number?" asked Daniel after he had finished off writing down the offer.

"Yes, yes, please call me back."

"Good-bye, Mr. Peabody."

Daniel hung up the phone and called Bryan Keller, the owner of the property.

"Yes, Daniel, what can I do for you?" asked Bryan Keller.

"Mr. Peabody called. I assume that you have the water, mineral and other rights to the property that includes the mine?"

"Yes, I do, Daniel. According to my deed paperwork, the water, mineral and other rights that include the old mine are Addendum F."

"Before I tell you what Mr. Peabody counter-offered for your property, can you tell me what the Colorado State Geologist's Office report said was in that mine?"

"Yeah. A copy of what is allegedly in the mine is attached to my deed. The mine's original filing is wax sealed from the Colorado State Geologist's Office in Denver, Colorado. In 1922, the mine allegedly contained high grade Silver, Gold, Tellurium and Molybdenum ores."

"Keep that original seal. The counter-offer is 125K more for the property. 150K more for the mineral, water and other rights and 120K for my lawyer's fees and time. What do you think?"

"I accept. That gives me 230K more in my pocket."

"Good. Let me call him back and inform him that the offer is accepted."

"Good-bye."

Daniel sealed the deal between the two of them. Mr. Peabody said he could see Daniel on Wednesday of the following week. As Daniel hung up the phone, Kim stepped into the office.

"Do you have your notepad, pen and video camera ready to go?" asked Daniel.

"Yes, Daniel. The video camera is charging up right now. It should be ready to go by Monday."

"Good. I'll call you when I receive the official notice to go tour the crime scene and the arrest scene; have a good weekend."

"You too, Daniel," she said as she left.

"Lynn, would you get me a demographics copy of the 6th Judicial District Jury Pool? I want to know how many different ethnicities we have here."

"Will do."

Daniel sat back down at his desk and did some paperwork. Just before closing time, Lynn printed up the demographics of the 6th Judicial District Jury Pool. Daniel looked at the pie chart and noticed that there was a disproportionate amount of Caucasians at 72%. African-Americans were next at 18%. The rest of the make up was a combination of 1% to 2% Hispanic, Native American, Alaskan Eskimo and Puerto Ricans. Daniel set the demographics pie chart down on the desktop.

"Lynn, do we have any electronic copies of the Change of Venue Request in accordance with Colorado Revised Statutes Title 16, Article 6, Parts 101 through 201?" asked Daniel.

"Yes, I have a dummy copy on my computer," she replied.

"Good. Get back in here after you lock up the front door and put the 'Closed' sign in the window."

Lynn grabbed her notepad and locked up the door after placing the 'Closed' sign in the window. Daniel dictated to her what he wanted to say in the Change of Venue Request. He made sure that he cited at least four U.S. Supreme Court cases as well as numerous lower court cases. He finished off with some Colorado State Supreme Court cases. She typed up the form and handed it to Daniel. He reviewed it and made some minor changes to the document. He then handed the document back to Lynn.

"Lynn, be sure to print up two copies and leave them unsigned. We will both go to the Ironton Community Bank on Monday and have both copies notarized," said Daniel as he put on his heavy jacket and proceeded out the door after he unlocked it.

Daniel watched as Lynn relocked the door, activated the alarm system and stepped into her car. Daniel knew she lived in Telluride and that it was going to be a long drive for her, especially during the winter months. He started driving down to Silverton where he lived.

Along the way, the Ironton Town Marshal's police vehicle went screaming passed him with the lights and siren going. Daniel pulled over to the side of the road to let the marshal go by. As he started to head out of town again, he saw that the Ironton Town Marshal's police vehicle was parked outside of Kim's office. Daniel pulled into the curb and stepped out of his car.

The Assistant Ironton Town Marshal, Julie Halverston, had put Kim in handcuffs and was putting her into the backseat of the police vehicle. Julie shut the door and went upstairs to gather evidence and take some pictures with the digital camera the police department had purchased a few years ago.

Daniel walked over to the police vehicle and tapped on the driver's side, rear window. Kim looked up and saw it was Daniel. Daniel could tell she had been in some sort of scuffle. Julie came down the stairs and yelled at Daniel.

"Get away from the police vehicle and away from the prisoner!" she yelled.

Daniel stepped away from the window.

"What happened?" asked Daniel as the sun was setting behind the mountains.

"She destroyed her own office, claimed she caught an intruder in her place of business and discharged three or four rounds from her firearm at the person," said Julie as she held up an evidence bag with spent shell casings, one live round, the magazine from Kim's weapon and the weapon itself. Daniel looked at everything carefully.

"Did she say anything else to you?" asked Daniel as he put the last evidence bag down on the hood of the police vehicle.

"Nothing except for her name, date of birth, address, occupation, etc. Any other questions I asked were answered with 'not without my lawyer present.'"

"Well now, her lawyer is present; shall we?" asked Daniel pointing to the stairs that led up to Kim's Private Investigations business.

"After you, counselor," replied Julie as she followed Daniel up the stairs.

CHAPTER 4

Daniel reached the top of the stairs first. He heard the burglar/fire/security alarm going off and found the door slightly ajar. He withdrew a pen from his jacket pocket and pushed the door open with it. The lights were on and Daniel did a quick look around before turning his attention to the alarm that was still going off.

The alarm was both audible, with an ear piercing, warbling noise and visual with alternating strobes. Daniel used the same pen to enter the alarm disarm code to silence the sound and the strobe lights. Julie shook her head in disbelief as Daniel put the pen back into his jacket pocket.

"Why did you do that maneuver with your pen just now?" she asked, pointing at the door and then the alarm keypad.

"There is a possibility that the perpetrator's fingerprints are all over the place in here. I didn't want to add any more fingerprints to the crime scene as it would make positively identifying the perpetrator a lot more difficult," said Daniel, smiling.

Daniel had a chance now to look around the place. Furniture had been overturned. The filing cabinet drawers emptied of their contents, which were now strewn throughout the floor of the business. Kim's desk had been overturned as well. The drawers pulled out and their contents added to the contents on the floor. Seat cushions from the couch and chairs had been destroyed leaving their interior components littered all over the floor and walls. Even the coffee stand had been wrecked.

"Who do you think did this and why?" asked Daniel as he looked at the broken glass next to the door and the pry marks on the doorjamb and frame. The smell of cordite was faintly apparent. Daniel looked around one last time and noticed that only a few things had been touched and touched professionally.

"As to why, I don't know. As to whom, an amateur. They were probably looking for something to steal and pawn or sell later for drug money. How am I doing so far, counselor?" asked Julie.

"I don't buy any of it. This room was made to look like an amateur did this. It was staged to look like this so that you wouldn't look any further into the issue," said Daniel flatly.

"So, if I dust for fingerprints, you don't think I will find any?"

"Oh, you'll find some fingerprints, but those fingerprints will probably be traced back to my client and her clients."

"You think this was done by a professional?"

"Probably wore leather gloves. I'm going back downstairs and talk to my client; don't you move. By the way, where did you find those spent shell casings?" asked Daniel.

"Over here," replied Julie, tapping her right foot on a section of the floor that had little markers on them with numbers.

"Okay. Will you please be kind enough to unlock the vehicle door? Are you planning on charging my client with anything, Marshal Halverston?"

"I plan on charging your client with Disorderly Conduct, Colorado Revised Statutes 18-9-106, Section 1, Subparagraph E, Not being a peace officer, discharges a firearm in a public place except when engaged in lawful target practice or hunting and causes property damage."

"What property damage is my client accused of doing?" asked Daniel as he looked at Julie and then past her to the open, back door that led into the San Juan National Forest.

"There is a bullet hole in the wall next to the backdoor."

"Very well," said Daniel as he turned and went down the stairs.

He spoke to Kim who told him what happened. She remembered that the person had worn gloves and tried to get passed her using the letter opener as a weapon. By the time Kim was through giving her statement, Marshal Beckman had arrived on the scene. He stepped out of another police vehicle and walked over to Daniel. Marshal Beckman was carrying a large, black, leather bag.

"Marshal Beckman, good to see you. Will you please remove the handcuffs from my client?" asked Daniel, smiling.

"After I talk to my associate upstairs," replied Jason.

Daniel waited in his car for another forty-five minutes before he saw Julie come down the stairs. She ambled towards his car. Daniel stepped slowly out of his vehicle so that he didn't alarm her.

"Mind coming upstairs, Daniel? Marshal Beckman has some questions for you," said Julie, smiling.

"Sure, not a problem," said Daniel, locking up his car.

Daniel followed Julie upstairs. The place was still in shambles. Daniel knocked on the doorframe. Marshal Beckman turned around as he put the digital camera back into the bag he had carried up earlier. The bag looked heavier and appeared larger than Daniel had remembered earlier. The sun had finally set and Daniel could see his, Julie's and Jason's breaths in the cold room. The lights were on so Daniel could see the room better now. Jason turned to face Daniel.

"Daniel, my associate here tells me you think that this burglary was staged, as you called it, is that correct?" asked Jason, almost ready to laugh.

"Yes, Marshal Beckman. A professional, making it look like an amateur had done it, really committed this burglary. You probably won't find any fingerprints anywhere because the perpetrator was wearing leather or vinyl exam type gloves," said Daniel as he looked around at the walls and floor.

"Okay, so the burglar wore gloves. I can still charge your client with Disorderly Conduct, 18-9-106, Section 1, Subparagraph E," said Jason, pointing to the bullet hole in the back doorframe.

"Not so fast, Marshal Beckman. My client had every right under Colorado Revised Statutes, 18-1-704.5, Section 2, Subparagraph B, to use deadly force on the intruder."

"Why did she have to shoot the burglar? Why not order the burglar to the floor and wait for us?" asked Jason.

"Did you find a letter opener by any chance?"

"Yes, about two feet from the desk; why?" asked Jason, showing it to Daniel.

"I'll bet you that the burglar charged at my client with that letter opener in his or her hands. I would say that letter opener is about 10 inches in length, isn't it?"

"Yeah, does that make a difference?" asked Julie.

"That makes one, ugly, edged weapon. I'm sure the duty DA for the 6th Judicial District would probably classify the letter opener as a deadly weapon under Colorado Revised Statutes, 18-1-901, Section 3, Subparagraphs IV and V."

"You don't need the DA's help on this one, counselor. I would consider a 10-inch long letter opener a deadly weapon. Mind telling me what you think happened?"

"Okay, after Marshal Halverston here goes down to her police vehicle and obtains my client's cell phone."

"Go get the cell phone," said Jason.

Julie left and returned a short time later with the cell phone. She handed the cell phone to Jason.

"Marshal Beckman, I think this is what may have happened. My client left my office at about 5:17 pm. She probably arrived at her office here at about 5:20 pm. She stepped out of her vehicle and headed upstairs towards her office/business here. She probably walked about half way up the stairs when she saw the flashing strobe lights and then, a few seconds later, she heard the audible part of the alarm system going off."

"So far, so good; go on," said Jason as he took some notes as well as recording the statements being made.

"She pulled out her cell phone and called your office directly. I'm going to guess that the call to your office went out about 5:22 pm. If you check the last outgoing number dialed, it is more than likely date and time stamped."

Jason flipped open the cell phone. The last outgoing phone call was to the Ironton Town Marshal's office. The time stamp was 5:23 pm. Jason looked up at Daniel.

"How am I doing so far, Marshal Beckman?" asked Daniel.

"You're a minute off so far. The call went out at 5:23 pm."

"Okay, so I missed the phone call by a minute. Now, my client knows that either you or Julie is in route and all she has to do is wait for one of you to show up."

"Go on, I'm still listening and taking notes," said Jason.

"I'm going to guess that at some point during the response time of, this is only a guess, nine minutes because of road conditions, the burglar exits the front door which he or she had forced open earlier," said Daniel, pointing at the pry marks on the doorframe and doorjamb.

"If I catch this burglar, what do you want them charged with?" asked Jason, trying to throw Daniel off the tracks.

Daniel was quick on his feet.

"First Degree Criminal Trespass, Colorado Revised Statutes 18-4-502, Second Degree Burglary, Colorado Revised Statutes 18-4-203, or, at the very least, Possession of Burglary Tools, Colorado Revised Statutes 18-4-205."

"Go on," said Jason still taking notes.

"My client probably never saw the burglar's face and when the burglar saw my client, they ran back inside. They probably saw the letter opener as the first weapon of choice to try and cut their way out of this place. My client, probably jacked up on adrenaline, stormed up the stairs and kicked open the already ajar door."

"Sounds plausible enough; go on," said Julie this time.

"I'm going to guess that by the time Julie arrived on scene, everything inside was done; i.e. the shooting. Since Julie didn't find anyone in the area right away, she arrested my client and is going to probably charge my client with Disorderly Conduct, 18-9-106, Section 1, Subparagraph E and maybe even False Reporting to Authorities, Colorado Revised Statutes 18-8-111, for the emergency call to your office."

"Any defense for your client, counselor?" asked Julie as she looked down in her ticket book. She had actually charged Kim with both offenses.

"Yes, as a small business owner, she has every right to protect herself, her clients and her business with any amount of force up to and including deadly force against an intruder. My client probably confronted the burglar as she rolled into the room here. Now, remember, both my client and the burglar are jacked up on adrenaline."

"So, what you're saying is, Kim has now confronted the burglar. That's not such a wise thing for her to do. I'm going to guess that next you're going to tell me that she and the burglar got into a fight of some kind," said Julie.

"Precisely, Marshal Halverston. Now, its letter opener versus my client's Springfield Armory, .45ACP. I'm going to guess that the burglar probably charged at my client using the letter opener in a very aggressive and threatening manner such as a slashing, cutting or stabbing motion. The burglar was probably trying to get out the front door, which my client was blockading at the time. At this point, my client opened fire on the burglar in self-defense."

"Then what happened?" asked Jason.

"My client fired one round which probably missed the burglar by mere millimeters, hence the bullet hole in the back door frame," said Daniel, pointing at the bullet hole.

"My client probably then charged at the burglar in fear of her life. The burglar was probably exiting the back door with the letter opener still being held in a threatening manner at my client. I'm going to guess that the burglar charged one last time at my client. The burglar then decided to throw the letter opener at my client."

"Okay, so far you've filled in the opportunity and jeopardy part of the equation, but the ability portion of the equation is a little weak," said Jason, still taking notes.

"My client, more than likely, tripped over something on the floor. This was in response to being charged at, assaulted, kicked, whatever. Or, maybe my client was just simply trying to get out of the way, duck or whatever you want to call it, Marshal Beckman. Either way, my client believed that she was going to receive great bodily injury or even die at the object coming at her."

"Okay, the ability portion of the equation is present now; please go on, this is making for a very interesting report that I'm sure the duty DA for the 6th Judicial District will love to read," said Julie. Jason chuckled a little bit as well.

"She probably fell onto the floor and if you look her over, Marshal Halverston, you will probably find Kim has bruises on her arms, legs, stomach and face. Those marks probably came from the burglar when he or she assaulted my client in an attempt to get out of this place."

"How come she missed with her first shot if the target was so close to her?" asked Jason.

"Probably the adrenaline dump caused the first shot to go awry. Remember, my client isn't held to as high a degree for her training as you two are."

"Very true, counselor," said Julie.

"I don't think she missed with shots two and three. Unfortunately, the burglar has been on the run for over two and quarter hours and is probably in Utah by now," said Daniel, looking at his watch.

"What makes you think the burglar is gone? Why not be waiting outside to come back?" asked Julie, suspiciously.

"Simple. The last time it snowed was December 29th of last year. If my client hit the person, there should be blood drops on the stairs and into the snow surrounding the bottom of the stairs. Trust me, the burglar has fled. I know that I would if I were shot at by the homeowner/business owner."

"You know that private investigators are not regulated in this state, right?" asked Jason.

"That's right, Marshal Beckman. Colorado is the only state in the union that doesn't regulate them. However, my client went through an accredited, Colorado based, private investigation school and has registered her business with the Colorado Secretary of State."

"So, where is her business license?" asked Julie.

"Hanging rather crookedly on the wall behind you, Marshal Halverston," said Daniel, pointing to an eight by ten picture frame, with shattered glass in the frame, which held the business license for Kim's business.

"Anything else, counselor?" asked Jason.

"Several things, Marshal Beckman. I want my client out of those handcuffs and brought up here so that she can tell you what is missing."

"What else?" asked Jason as he motioned for Julie to go get Kim.

"I want my client checked out by Doctor Tills in Silverton. I also want my client's property returned to her."

"I will do all those things after I talk to your client and, just to make sure that you don't contaminate your client's statement to me, you go wait in your car," said Jason.

"Fair enough, Marshal Beckman," said Daniel.

Daniel left the room as Kim was brought into the room. Daniel went to his car and turned on the engine. He turned on the heater a few seconds later and waited. Another thirty minutes passed before he saw Jason coming down the stairs. Kim was with him and Daniel saw that Kim was out of the handcuffs. Jason knocked on the driver's side window. Daniel rolled the window down.

"You're lucky, Daniel. This is only the fourth time in my 25-year career in law enforcement that the client's statement and the lawyer's statement were almost identical."

"Then my client is free to go?" asked Daniel.

"Yes, she is free to go. I called Doctor Tills for you and he is waiting for the both of you in his office," said Jason.

"Thank you, Marshal Beckman. I would like to get a copy of your police report, investigation notes and crime scene photos, please."

"Fat chance, counselor. Those items are evidence; have a safe trip."

"Thank you."

Daniel rolled up his window. He waited until after law enforcement had left before he spoke to Kim.

"Go upstairs and get a couple of changes of clothes; it's not safe for you here tonight. Turn your thermostat down to sixty-five degrees. Grab your gun cleaning kit and spare ammunition," said Daniel.

"Okay."

Kim left and went upstairs to pack. When she had returned, Daniel drove her to see Doctor Tills. Doctor Tills gave Kim some painkillers for her bruising. Daniel took her back to his place for the night. Daniel slept downstairs in the basement while Kim slept upstairs in the loft. The next morning, Daniel fixed them both breakfast after he had worked out and showered. He then drove her back to her business. It was daylight now. As they entered the room, Daniel looked at Kim.

"You told me last night, the only things that the burglar took were the laser range-finder, the video camera and some blank video tapes, right?" asked Daniel.

"That's right," said Kim as she started cleaning up the place.

"Then it wasn't a simple burglary. Someone was looking for something they thought we had or might find out," said Daniel.

"Well, I'll have to buy some new equipment," said Kim.

"Use my business credit card and go to either Denver or Durango; get the good stuff," said Daniel, handing her the credit card.

"Will do," she said, taking it.

Daniel started looking around and found some strange spots on the back stairs, the railing and in the snow at the bottom of the stairs. He ran down to his car and grabbed a piece of equipment he had bought years ago for hunting. He grabbed his blood detector. He ran the blood detector over the spots and they glowed a bright blue. Daniel called Marshal Beckman. As Daniel waited for Marshal Beckman to arrive, he saw Kim drive off safely.

"Daniel, you called me about finding some bloodstains?" asked Jason.

"Yes. I found them over by the railing at the back door and at the bottom of the stairs where they are the heaviest," replied Daniel.

"I didn't find any last night. Are you sure those bloodstains are human and not animal? How long have they been there?"

"I don't think the bloodstains are animal, I think they're human. They are fresh, because they're still a little bit red. They aren't brown."

"I'll go check it out and thanks for the call counselor; you're free to go."

When Jason had let Daniel go, he drove towards home. As Daniel scanned the road ahead, he looked to his right at San Juan Forest Service Road 881. Daniel saw that the Colorado Department of Transportation snowplow had been down the main road he was on only a few days ago. The snowplow had pushed the snow over the entrance to the forest service road blocking it.

There were tracks in the plowed snow. Daniel stopped his car, got out and walked up the road. The tracks were tire tracks of a vehicle. After walking about a half a mile up the road, in knee-deep snow, Daniel found the vehicle that had made the tracks. As Daniel approached the car, he could see that the driver's side window was rolled down.

"Hello?" said Daniel loudly.

Daniel cautiously walked up to the driver's side of the car.

"Hello? Are you alright?" asked Daniel loudly, once again. This time, Daniel cautiously touched the driver's right shoulder.

There was no response of any kind, so Daniel stepped in front of the car to look at the driver. The eyes of the driver were staring blankly in Daniel's direction. Daniel began waving his right hand up and down to check for any type of reaction from the driver; there was no reaction by the driver. Cautiously, he walked back over to the driver's side of the car.

Daniel had found a body out there on that forest service road. He reached down to feel for a pulse on the neck of the driver; no pulse. Daniel pulled his cell phone out of his jacket pocket and called the San Juan County Sheriffs Office.

CHAPTER 5

Daniel gave his statement to the deputy sheriff that arrived on scene. Soon the San Juan County Coroner arrived on the scene. She drove the four-wheel drive coroner's vehicle down the unplowed forest service road to where the sheriff's deputy had marked off the car with crime scene tape. She exited the vehicle and put on vinyl exam gloves to begin a basic assessment of how the person may have died.

Nabiya then recruited the help of the sheriff's deputy to assist her with putting the body into a body bag. They both put the body in the back of the vehicle. The deputy then drove to the front of the forest service road to await the tow truck. Nabiya walked up the road towards Daniel.

"Have any idea who he is?" asked Nabiya, taking off her exam gloves that Daniel could see were covered in blood.

"Not a clue. He may be the burglar that Kim shot and that Marshal Beckman is looking for," said Daniel.

"Being shot explains the two-bullet holes I found in him."

"Make sure that Marshal Beckman knows about the two bullet holes in the corpse. I think, when you do the autopsy, you might find that the two bullets you remove will match Kim's .45ACP."

"Do you know, by any chance, what type of bullets she uses?"

"I believe she uses Winchester, 230 grain, SXT® rounds."

"Thank you, counselor," she said as she walked back to her vehicle. She said something to the deputy as she turned her vehicle, with the body in the back, towards Silverton.

The deputy sheriff walked over to where Daniel was standing.

"You're free to go, counselor," said the deputy.

"Thank you, deputy," replied Daniel.

Daniel stepped back into his vehicle and drove home. Very late that night, Kim returned with new equipment and the receipts. The next morning, Daniel drove her back to her office. Kim taped over the broken window with some silver tape. She then turned up the heat a little. Daniel turned to her.

"When you fired those other two shots, were you standing, kneeling or prone?" he asked.

"Kneeling, facing the back door," she said to him, showing her position.

"I thought so. Keep your .45 handy, and I'll see you on Wednesday at the office," said Daniel as he left.

"Good-bye," she said, looking at him strangely.

Daniel arrived at the office early Monday morning. He checked his phone messages first. There were the usual ones asking about fees and advice. There was one question in those ten messages that he had about suing a funeral home for something. The last message was from Linda. Daniel poured himself a cup of coffee and dialed Linda's number.

"Hello, Daniel, I heard your private investigator's place of business was disassembled this past Friday night. I understand she shot the intruder, is that correct?" asked Linda, gleefully.

"Yes, that is correct, Linda. However, law enforcement needs to invest in the 911 system up here."

"My understanding is, law enforcement does have the 911 system up there. By the way, I read both your statement and the statement from your private investigator about what happened. Just to make you happy, I will drop the pending charges against her."

"Thank you, Linda. Is there anything else?"

"Yes, I understand you found a corpse this weekend as well. Mind telling me about it?"

"Yes, I did find a corpse this weekend. Boy, you and Marshal Beckman must be really good friends or are you and the San Juan County Sheriffs Department. or maybe the San Juan County Coroner, good friends?"

"Have any idea who he was?" she asked, evading the question Daniel had just asked.

"Not a clue. I was hoping that you could tell me."

"Fat chance. I still don't have the autopsy report or the fingerprint identification back yet."

"Can I ask for a professional favor, then?" asked Daniel politely.

"What do you want?"

"Either a seizure warrant or a subpoena duces tecum for the alleged burglary notes, the photos and the investigation notes for said alleged burglary on Friday night. Marshal Beckman has been a little uncooperative."

"I'll get Judge Kyle Tillman to sign the subpoena duces tecum, is that okay?"

"Sounds fine to me."

"Oh, I'm faxing the San Juan County Sheriffs Department your permission slip to tour the crime scene. They should be calling you shortly."

"Thank you."

"Good-bye."

Daniel turned around and called Kim to let her know about touring the crime scene. She told Daniel she would be ready to go. Daniel looked up as the door opened. Lynn was walking into the outer office. She turned on her computer and took off her heavy jacket, hanging it up on the wall mounted coat rack. She then went about her regular office duties.

When the actual time came to open, Juan walked into the office with Roberto. Juan had a small, dark blue book in his right hand. Lynn asked Juan and Roberto to have a seat while she walked into Daniel's inner office.

"Daniel, Juan is here with Roberto and I think he has his passport," she said.

"Good. Call the DA's office and tell them that my client has his passport and will surrender it in accordance with the terms named at the arraignment. They need to bring a seizure warrant with them."

"Will do."

A few minutes later the phone started ringing. Since Lynn was busy with other things, Daniel answered the phone.

"Attorney Daniel Marcos' office, how can I help you?" asked Daniel.

"Yes, is Attorney Daniel Marcos there?" asked the voice.

"Speaking," said Daniel.

"Daniel, this is Trooper Davis. We met a few months ago during a most unusual trial."

"Oh, yes, the drunken sheriff you arrested. What can I do for you?"

"I don't know exactly where the Ironton Town Marshal's office is located."

"I'll meet you there. Take Highway 550 to Silverton. Turn left off the highway onto Main Street. Follow Main Street for four miles. You will see my office on the left and the Town Marshal's office on your right at about five miles."

"Thank you and I will see you there in ten minutes."

"I'll see you there."

Daniel hung up the phone and headed out the door as he grabbed his heavy jacket.

"Juan and Roberto, I have to run across the street to the Town Marshal's office; I'll be right back. When I get back, I want to talk to you, Juan."

"Yes, sir."

Daniel walked over to the Town Marshal's office. He arrived at almost the same time as Trooper Davis. They greeted each other and walked into Jason's office. Jason stood up as they walked inside his office ever mindful of the low ceiling.

"Good morning, counselor. What's this I hear you told the DA's office that we don't have the 911 system up here?"

"We don't have 911 for cell phones up here, yet. If you call 911 from your cell phone, the call goes to the nearest Colorado State Patrol office. In this case the closest office is Durango. There, the state patrol dispatcher has to transfer the call to the appropriate county sheriff's dispatcher. Then, if the call is specific to, say, you, Marshal Beckman, the call has to be transferred again; too much time is wasted."

"I see. Trooper Davis, is that statement true?" asked Jason.

"Yes, in regards to cell phones. However, if you call 911 from a landline, unless you're outside the city limits of the town you're calling from, the call gets sent directly to you, sir. However, if you're outside the city limits, the call goes to the county sheriff's office. Also, if you call 911 from the 911 emergency phones located at most rest areas, the call goes to the Colorado Highway Patrol."

"Thank you, Trooper Davis. What can I do for you two?" asked Jason.

"This subpoena duces tecum is for you," said Trooper Davis, handing Jason the paperwork.

Jason took the paperwork and looked it over. He set the paperwork down on his desktop and walked over to some filing cabinets in the left corner of the office. He used one of his keys to unlock the filing cabinet. He then pulled out a large, manila colored envelope from the drawer and closed it back up. Jason handed Daniel the envelope.

"Something told me you might pull a stunt like this," said Jason.

"Well, if you had been a bit more cooperative than what you were, this whole situation could have been avoided," said Daniel, taking the envelope with him and leaving the office.

Daniel returned to his office. He made sure that a copy of the seizure warrant for Juan's passport was made part of the case file. Juan walked into Daniel's office, closed the door and sat down in a chair that was directly in front of Daniel. Daniel called Lynn into the office and had her take notes. Daniel asked Juan a lot of questions. Around lunchtime, Juan left Daniel's office.

When Lynn had typed up Juan's deposition, Daniel had her make a copy for Linda. Lynn sent it to Linda via Certified Mail® with return receipt. After lunch, Daniel received a large package in the mail. Lynn opened up the package and removed the contents.

"Daniel, we just received the autopsy photos, coroner's notes, police notes and reports and the crime scene photos," said Lynn taking the stack of stuff into Daniel's office.

"Good. Call Jessica; get her to come over to the office right now. No ballistics report?"

"No, I didn't see the ballistics report in there; okay," said Lynn as the phone started ringing.

Lynn answered the phone. She took down a quick note and hung up the phone. She walked back into Daniel's office and handed him the message.

"Judge Bishop wants to see you in his private chambers in Silverton as soon as possible," said Lynn.

"And I'll bet you it's about the Change of Venue request. Tell Jessica to start going over the crime scene photos while I'm gone."

"Good luck."

"Thank you, I'm going to need it."

Daniel left the office and drove to Silverton. He parked down the street from the Silverton Courthouse and walked inside. After passing through the metal detector and other security measures, he entered Judge Bishop's outer office. His secretary smiled as Daniel entered the office.

"I'm here to see Judge Bishop in regards to a Change of Venue request I submitted. He called me a few minutes ago."

"Go ahead on inside His Honor's private chambers; they have been expecting you Mr. Marcos Esquire," she said.

Daniel walked into the judge's private chambers. He closed the door and turned around to see two other judges in the chambers. Daniel looked at Judge Kyle Tillman and smiled. Judge Kyle Tillman smiled back at him. Daniel had to study the face of the female judge in the chambers a few seconds before he realized who it was. The other person was Associate Justice Jil Bergman of the Colorado State Supreme Court. They all shook hands as Daniel remained standing.

"Daniel, I received your Change of Venue request; please have a seat," said Larry, pointing at a chair in front of his desk. Daniel sat down.

"Thank you, Your Honor," said Daniel, looking at Judge Kyle Tillman and Associate Justice Bergman.

"I believe you know Judge Kyle Tillman here," said Larry, pointing to his right.

"Yes, I do, Your Honor," said Daniel politely.

"Good to see you Daniel," said Judge Kyle Tillman.

"Do you know who is sitting to my left?" asked Larry.

"I believe, Your Honor, that is Associate Justice Jil Bergman of the Colorado State Supreme Court. She was a guest speaker at the Denver University Law School many times during my stay there. Good to see you, Your Honor," said Daniel.

"Good to see you, Daniel," she said, coyly.

"I called this meeting of the other judges to discuss your Change of Venue request. I know that a three judge panel is not necessary, but I wanted this hearing to be as fair and impartial as possible."

"Thank you, Your Honor, I appreciate your integrity in this matter."

"First question, do you, at this time, request that I recuse myself from this trial in accordance with Colorado Revised Statutes 16-6-201, covering this issue?" asked Larry.

"No, Your Honor. I believe that at the preliminary hearing, I was able to clearly establish that my client was indeed a U.S. citizen and would probably not run away."

"So you did. Second question, if the Change of Venue request is denied, would you protest and why, or why not?"

"I would have to protest the denial of the request, Your Honors. My client's 5th, 6th and 14th Amendment rights would be severely violated."

"In what way, exactly?" asked Jil as she looked over her copy of the Change of Venue request.

"My client's 5th and 14th Amendment rights under due process would be violated in that, by not allowing the Change of Venue, in accordance with Colorado Revised Statutes, my client would not receive a fair trial in this judicial district."

"You mentioned, in your Change of Venue request, that your client's rights under the 6th Amendment would be violated as well. Please explain that one," said Judge Kyle Tillman.

"My client has a right under both the 6th Amendment to the U.S. Constitution and the Colorado Constitution, to a trial by a jury of his or her peers. There are almost no Hispanics, Native Americans etc. in this judicial district. In my Change of Venue request statement, I listed several U.S. Supreme Court cases in which the person appealing their conviction did so on the basis that their trial was biased against them in some manner."

"You did list several U.S. Supreme Court cases with which I am very familiar with all but one of them. Would you please explain this one that is listed in your statement?" asked Jil, pointing to the first case listed.

"That particular case was the first time that the U.S. Supreme Court ruled that the wording of the 6th Amendment, in this case the sentence of 'by an impartial jury of the State and district wherein the crime shall have been committed' meant that the jury had to be made up people like the defendant."

"I believe, Your Honors, I now know which case he is referring to; what year was this case?" asked Jil.

"I believe the year was 1924. The defendant was arrested for burglary, tried and convicted of his crime. He appealed his conviction to the State of Mississippi's Supreme Court, which refused to hear the case. The case was passed to the U.S. Supreme Court in 1926, where the U.S. Supreme Court overturned his conviction for a variety of reasons."

"Go on," she said, listening intently.

"The U.S. Supreme Court ruled that an all white jury, a white judge, a white prosecutor and a white public defender, had violated the wording of the 6th Amendment. They based their decision on, I believe, the fact that when the Court asked for a copy of the jury pool from the district where the crime and trial occurred in, the jury pool showed almost all whites. The defendant was an African-American male and with almost no African-American males or females in the jury pool, the conviction was overturned and the person was exonerated of his crime."

"Excellent, Daniel," she said, smiling broadly.

"We are all familiar with the Colorado State Supreme Court cases you listed; good job," said Judge Kyle Tillman.

"Thank you, Your Honor. When can I expect an answer, then?" asked Daniel expectantly.

"After we do further legal review, Daniel. I will have to take the request back to Denver with me. The Chief Justice of the Colorado State Supreme court will have the final say," said Jil, who winked her right eye at Daniel.

"I understand, Your Honor."

"If the Change of Venue request is granted, where would you want the trial moved to?" asked Larry.

"Either Grand Junction or Durango would be sufficient."

"Dismissed, Daniel," said Larry.

Daniel stood up and shook everybody's hands once again. He returned to his office where he sat down and started going over the crime scene and autopsy photos. After dinner, Daniel sent everyone home. He drove home himself, worked out on his home gym and went to bed.

CHAPTER 6

The next morning found Daniel at the office just before opening time. Mr. Peabody, the assistant to Mr. Peabody and Mr. Keller were already waiting for him. All parties involved were very eager to sign the paperwork. As the paperwork was signed and notarized by the assistant to Mr. Peabody, the checks were exchanged. Daniel looked at his check and smiled. When Lynn came in, Daniel had her go to the bank with the check to deposit it into the account. As Mr. Keller was leaving, Daniel stopped him.

"Mr. Keller, who owns the property to your southwest corner?" asked Daniel.

"A fellow by the name of Roy Georgeton. Doesn't like visitors calling and I understand he has built himself his own shooting range at the far end of the property."

"Thank you, Mr. Keller," said Daniel as Lynn returned.

Lynn walked into the office with an envelope. The envelope had a green cover to it. She handed it to Daniel, who opened it up. The letter contained the official letterhead stamp from the office of the Chief Justice of the Colorado State Supreme Court. Daniel read the letter and then put it down on the desktop.

"Did the court grant the request?" asked Lynn.

"No. This letter is merely a confirmation of receipt of the request. The court has assigned my request docket number 11-226. We should receive an official reply to the request in ten days."

"Daniel, I believe that the court will grant the request."

Daniel didn't say anything; he only smiled instead.

"Lynn, put this in Juan's file," said Daniel as he picked up the letter and handed it to her.

"Do we need to send a copy to Linda?"

"No. The CC on the letter said she would receive a copy. Please bring me Juan's statement so that I can read it again."

"Yes, Daniel."

Lynn returned a few seconds later and handed the statement to Daniel. Daniel read the statement and made some mental notes. He poured himself a cup of coffee and handed the statement back to Lynn. The door opened and Jessica walked into the office.

"Jessica, let's go see the spot where my client was arrested for the shooting," said Daniel setting his cup of coffee down on a cup warmer that he bought from a client.

"Okay."

Both Daniel and Jessica drove out of town to where San Juan County Roads 18 and 281 intersected. They stopped the car they were riding in and exited the vehicle. They started looking around. Daniel saw that the house, where the two people had been shot to death, was visible from the area he was standing. Daniel noticed that the angle to the house appeared to be very steep.

"Jessica, do you have your laser range-finder with you?"

"Yes, it's in the car."

"Go get it and stand right here. Tell me how far it is to that object," said Daniel, pointing at the house.

Jessica left and returned with the range-finder. The new range-finder she had purchased was designed with minute of angle capabilities. She stood where Daniel had been standing and used the range-finder. She also had a small notepad and pen with her.

"180-yards/60-meters, up angle 35 degrees," she said.

"Good, write that down. Now, behind me is Juan's place. Stay here while I go to where the center of the road is located. I'm going to raise my right arm; range-find me."

"Okay, Daniel."

Daniel walked to where he thought the middle of the road was and raised his right arm. She wrote down the distance and angle. As Daniel walked back to Jessica, his cell phone rang.

"Hello?" asked Daniel.

"Daniel, its Lynn. I just had a San Juan County Sheriff's deputy in here at the office. She wants to meet you at the crime scene today at around 1:00 pm."

"Sounds good to me; thank you," said Daniel, hanging up the phone. Jessica walked over to him.

"Jessica, lets go get some lunch and we will get your video camera as well. I was just informed that we could tour the crime scene today around 1:00 pm."

"Sounds good to me, I'm hungry."

Jessica drove them both to the Ironton Café for lunch. After lunch, Jessica stopped by her office to pick up the video camera. They drove up San Juan County Road 281 to the crime scene. When they arrived at the crime scene, they saw the "CRIME SCENE—DO NOT ENTER" tape across the front door. There was also a San Juan County Sheriff's car parked in the driveway. The deputy stepped out of her vehicle to greet them.

"You must be Attorney at Law Daniel Marcos and you must be Mr. Marcos' private investigator, Jessica Kim," she said, smiling as she shook their hands.

"Yeah, we sure are. How did you know?" asked Daniel suspiciously.

"I pulled up your driver's license pictures on my onboard computer system."

"I see; shall we?" asked Daniel as they headed towards the door.

The deputy sheriff unlocked the door and then opened it up. She stood outside the door while they went inside and looked around. Jessica immediately started filming the crime scene. She carefully walked around as Daniel looked at where the two bodies were located when they had been shot. Daniel turned around to see that the lamp on the table by the door was crooked. The lamp was leaning towards the shot out window.

"Jessica, film this lamp carefully," said Daniel.

"Sure," she said filming it carefully from various angles.

Daniel turned to look at the couch. It was bloodstained heavily in one area. Daniel looked up towards the ceiling and then back down to the floor. There appeared to be no bloodstains on the carpet or the ceiling. That's when Daniel noticed a gouge in the armrest of the couch. He kneeled down to get a better look at it.

The gouge was in a direct line with the leaning lamp. Daniel motioned for Jessica to videotape this evidence. Daniel stood up and opened the door. There, just below the door latch was a gouge as well. He turned to face Jessica.

"Video this as well," he said, pointing at the spot near the door latch. He then went searching for the thermostat.

He found the thermostat on the inside, kitchen wall facing the living room. The thermostat read sixty-eight degrees. The house felt much colder than that, so Daniel assumed the needle on the thermostat didn't go any lower than sixty-eight degrees. Daniel, however, could see his breath as he walked back out into the living room. Jessica was video taping everything in the living room. Daniel looked up as the deputy sheriff stuck her head in the front door.

"Are you two about finished?" she asked.

"Almost. Deputy, do you have a gunshot residue test kit in your car by any chance?" asked Daniel.

"Yes, I have the nitrate QuickTest® Kit. Do we need to use this test kit?"

"I think so. Could you, please, use the test kit on this gouge on the couch, the leaning lamp and gouge just under the door latch. If you find the missing piece of the lamp, which I suspect you won't, test it."

"Sure. Personally, I don't think your client did it, Mr. Marcos."

The deputy went to her car and mixed up the chemicals from the test kit. She returned and used the cotton swab dabber and dabbed the places Daniel had asked to be tested. The deputy, as Daniel had suspected, didn't find the missing piece of the lamp. Jessica videotaped the deputy doing the test and then she pulled out her pen and notepad to take notes.

Jessica noted the test kit lot number, manufacturer, test date, person doing the test and expiration date of the test kit. The deputy threw out the rest of the test kit and returned. Daniel watched as the orange colored liquid placed on all those areas began changing color. In twenty minutes, the color was a bright green.

"Deputy, what color is considered a positive test?" asked Daniel.

"With that test kit, it turns from orange to bright green," she replied as she looked down at the bright green spots.

"Thank you, deputy. Will you please give Jessica your contact information; we will be leaving shortly."

"Sure."

Jessica videotaped the rest of the crime scene. Everyone left around 2:45 pm. Jessica dropped off her equipment at her office. Daniel told her to start typing up her notes into a formal statement. Daniel arrived back at the office to find Lynn opening up the mail. There was another Certified Mail® letter that she handed to him. Daniel took the letter back into his office, where he opened it. The letter was a copy of the ballistics report from the Colorado Bureau of Investigation.

Daniel poured himself a fresh cup of coffee and sat down at his desk. He read the ballistics technician's report. The report showed that three slugs total, with a fourth, partial bullet fragment, had been sent to the lab for analysis. The technician was able to match the slugs and fragment blood type with the deceased's through medical records. The fragment turned out to be a piece of bronze. The ballistics technician, Garth Smith, signed the report and made a notation in the comments field that caught Daniel's attention.

The notation said, "Bullets were too badly damaged for an exact match-up to the weapon provided by the Ironton Town Marshal's office for testing; bronze metal fragment inconsistent with known handgun rounds. Bullets were measured at between .429 inches in diameter to .456 inches in diameter. These diameters were measured at the base of the bullets." Daniel picked up the phone and called Linda.

"I want a dismissal of the charges against my client," said Daniel.

"No dice, counselor."

"The ballistics technician couldn't match the slugs to the gun provided for him to test."

"I saw the report. But, the blood type on the slugs matches the deceased."

"Of course the blood matches the deceased; the bullets passed through their bodies. Any idiot could see that, Linda. The slugs were too badly damaged."

"No dismissal, counselor; good-bye," she said, hanging up the phone.

Daniel hung up the phone, pursing his lips together to control his anger. He walked out into the outer office where Lynn was sitting.

"Get Juan on a conference call and get Jessica over here. I'm going to slam-dunk Linda."

"Okay."

Daniel went back into his office and closed the door. He sat down at his desk and started writing down some notes. Kim showed up and knocked on his door. Daniel put down the pen and opened the door.

Kim walked into the office and Daniel showed her one of three seats in the office that were to the left of his desk.

She opened up her notepad and took out a pen from the inside, left jacket pocket. Lynn walked in and looked at Daniel. She also had a notepad and Juan's case file, which contained all the evidence gathered so far. She sat down in a chair that was to the right of his desk.

"Juan is on line 1," said Lynn.

"Thank you. Put the 'CLOSED' sign in the window and lock the door."

"Okay."

She left and returned a few seconds later. She closed the door and sat back down. Daniel turned to face them as he picked up his notepad.

"Here's the situation. I read the copy of the ballistics technician's report and I tried to get Linda to drop the charges. She wouldn't drop the charges, so I've decided to slam-dunk her."

He paused a minute before he pushed the flashing lit button on the phone.

"Juan, this is your attorney, you're on a speakerphone so that my private investigator and my secretary can hear this part of the conversation. Is that alright with you?"

"Yes, sir."

"I know that you told me these answers to the questions I am about to ask in your formal statement to me, but I am going to ask these questions again. Where did you buy that gun you were arrested with and what make, model, and caliber specifically, is it?"

"I bought it on December 29th of 2010 at Gene Taylor's Sporting Goods store in Grand Junction."

"Was the transaction cash, check or charge?" asked Daniel.

"Cash. The gun was a 6-inch, Magnaport® barreled, Taurus, Model 44B6, .44 magnum."

"Is it blue or silver in color?" asked Daniel.

"It is blue, sir."

"What did you do after 6:00 pm on the night of the shooting?"

"Made some phone calls to relatives, bought a box of ammunition and went shooting into that hillside where I was arrested."

"Where did you buy that box of ammunition and what type of ammunition was it?" asked Daniel.

"I bought the last box of .44 Smith and Wesson Special, Silvertip® ammunition from a specialty store in Silverton. They didn't have any .44 magnum."

"Do you have a small game hunting license, by any chance?"

"Yes, in November of 2010, I went to Durango on some errands and bought a Colorado Resident Small Game Hunting and Fishing License Combo for about $55.00."

"Good. Do you own a four-wheel drive vehicle?"

"No, but my brother does."

"Did you go anywhere near that house the night of the shooting?"

"No, sir, I did not."

"Did anyone else, besides your brother, see you in that spot that night?"

"I remember several vehicles going by before midnight."

"Did you recognize any of the vehicles?"

"One belonged to the caretaker of the house where those people were murdered. One had an animal on the driver's side door. There was one I didn't recognize and one that I think belongs to Mr. Keller up the canyon."

"Good. Now, don't leave your house for any reason for the next few days."

"Okay, sir."

After Juan had hung up, Daniel started issuing his orders.

"Jessica, I want you to find out how many bullets and by what manufacturers are made of bronze. Also, find out how many handguns and rifles fire bullets from .429 inch diameter to .456 inch diameter."

"Yes, sir," she said as she tried to leave, but Daniel stopped her with a last minute request.

"Jessica, find out how many different rounds that a .44 magnum revolver can fire."

"Yes, Daniel," she said as she left.

"Lynn, find out exactly who owns the property to the southwest corner of Mr. Keller's property. Also, find out what hunting seasons are going on right now."

"Okay."

"Good-night Lynn, see you Monday morning."

CHAPTER 7

The alarm clock went off way too early Monday morning for Daniel. He rolled over and turned it off. He rolled back over and rubbed his eyes. He stretched out before working out on his home gym, before taking a shower. He ate breakfast and decided to walk to work. The four-mile jog from Silverton to Ironton, uphill and in freezing cold temperatures, helped him clear his head. He arrived at the office the same time as Lynn. They both walked inside after Lynn had disarmed the alarm.

Lynn turned on her computer and started a pot of coffee for the both of them as she picked up the morning edition of the *Ironton Gazette*. She tossed the newspaper on her desk and went to the post office to get the mail. She returned with the mail, set it down on her desktop and started checking phone messages. When she had finished checking phone messages, she opened the mail. Jessica walked into the outer office with all her information on the guns she had found. Daniel looked up and saw Jessica standing in his doorway.

"Come on in," he said.

Jessica entered Daniel's inner office and shut the door. She handed Daniel the stack of printouts. Daniel looked through it and handed it back to her.

"Make sure that Lynn makes a copy of these printouts. Anything of major interest?"

"Yes. At least two of those handguns on that list are capable of firing all of those bullet diameters listed on the ballistics report with only a simple change out of the barrel."

"Which ones?"

"A company called Thompson-Contender and Remington Arms Company with their Model XP-1100. They make single shot handguns that fire both handgun and rifle calibers."

"That's very good. What about the bullets?"

"I'm still researching that one. Right now, it appears Taurus and Remington are the only ones with current production lines."

"Get back to me on that issue."

"Will do. Oh, I found out that any current manufactured .44 magnum revolver can fire .44 Special and .44 Russian rounds as well. Older models, those that were made prior to, say, the mid 1960's, have to have what is called a fluted cylinder to fire those other rounds."

"Good work; get going," said Daniel as she left.

Jessica left and Lynn put the copies she made into an envelope. Lynn walked into Daniel's office with the envelope.

"Mark those as Defense Exhibits A1 through A12. Make sure that Linda gets a copy as well."

"Okay."

"Anything else?"

"We received our response to the Change of Venue Request," she said as she handed the green envelope to Daniel. She left the room as Daniel opened up the envelope and removed the letter.

The letterhead had the same familiar stamp from the Colorado State Supreme Court across the top of it. Daniel read the letter and smiled. The Change of Venue Request had been granted. Daniel walked out of the office and gave Lynn the letter.

"Put that letter into Juan's case file. Call Juan and inform him that the trial will be held in Mesa County. Find out when the Mesa County Courthouse can hold the trial."

"Yes, Daniel. What about Linda?"

"The letter states that a copy was forwarded to her. I will surmise that Linda will call me with the exact court date."

"That sounds reasonable."

Daniel poured himself a cup of coffee and went back into his office. He pulled out a legal pad and pen from his upper, right hand desk drawer. He began writing down his opening statements. Lynn stepped into his office and handed him a list of available court dates. The phone rang and Lynn answered it. The voice at the other end was brief. Lynn hung up the phone after taking the message down.

"That was Linda. She said that April 14th of this year would work for her. Court will start at 8:00 am each day. The Mesa County Sheriff's Department will only transport and house the prisoner if requested."

"Good. Call Juan and let him know."

"Okay."

Daniel looked up at the clock on the wall to the left of his desk; lunchtime. Lynn ate her lunch at her desk after she locked up the main entrance to the office. Daniel ate his lunch at the local café. He returned to find Lynn chatting with a Colorado Division of Wildlife person.

"Daniel, this is Wildlife Conservation Officer Dwight Odoms. He claims he saw our client on the night of the murder," said Lynn.

"That's wonderful news. Did you get a statement from him?" asked Daniel.

"Yes, Daniel."

Daniel looked over the man's uniform. He saw the animal symbol on the uniform.

"Mr. Odoms, my client told me he saw a truck with an animal on the side of if."

"It was me your client saw that night. I made sure that he was at least 50 feet off the centerline of the road in order to be discharging a firearm legally."

"Thank you, sir. If I need you as a witness for the defense, I will call you. Did you give Lynn, here, your contact information?"

"Yes, I did and I don't think your client did it either."

After Mr. Odoms had left, Daniel went into his office and tried to finish off his opening statement. As the afternoon dragged on, Lynn went to get the mail. She returned, opened up the dozen or so envelopes and began sorting them all out. Junk mail went into a box to be shredded later. She opened up the envelopes containing the monthly bills next.

It was the lonely envelope containing a letter from the Clerk of the Court for the 9th Federal Circuit Court covering the State of Arizona, which included the City of Nogales, that proved to be the most interesting. The letter was polite but short. Lynn filed the letter into Juan's case file and then paid the bills. After returning from the post office, Lynn walked into the office and knocked on Daniel's doorframe. Daniel looked up and put the pen and legal pad down on his desktop. He could tell something was on her mind.

"What's on your mind, Lynn?" asked Daniel.

"A very peculiar letter we received today. I've already filed the letter away in Juan's case file. The letter was in response to our request for more information on the INS raid you asked about."

"What did the court say?"

"The letter, from the Clerk of the Court for the 9th Federal Circuit Court, said that although the case had been adjudicated and everyone deported, the court case files, evidence, etc., were sealed; why?"

"Well, the most common reason is some sort of an on-going investigation with other law enforcement agencies. There's also a possibility that there is something in the record that can't be made public just yet."

"Oh well, silly of me to have asked."

Daniel smiled and then an idea snapped into his head.

"Good critical thinking skills, Lynn. It shows that you have the mind of a good, criminal defense attorney as well as being an excellent paralegal."

"Thank you, Daniel. By the way, only an officer of a court of law can look into a sealed court file, right?"

"Yes. The clerk of a court, a DA, a judge, etc., can look into such a record."

Daniel was quiet for a minute before continuing.

"Lynn, type up a letter to Her Honor Krysta Johnson."

"What does this letter need to say?" she asked as she grabbed a pen from her desk and a small notepad from her upper, right desk drawer.

"Ask Her Honor for a list of the INS agents that were involved with the raid. I also want a list of the deportee's names; specifically, I want to know if my client's parents were among those deported."

"Will do."

"Inform Her Honor that we would like the information by April 5th, if possible."

Lynn left the office and typed up the rough draft of the letter. She took it into Daniel for review. After he made some minor changes, she retyped the letter. Daniel signed off on it and Lynn both mailed and faxed the letter. When Lynn had returned from the post office, Jessica walked up behind her. Lynn turned around to face Jessica who was carrying a large load of paperwork.

"Hello, Jessica, here let me help you with all that paperwork," said Lynn, grabbing some of the paperwork.

"Thanks; is Daniel here?"

"Yes, he is in his inner office."

"Thank you."

Jessica walked into Daniel's inner office. She and Lynn set down the multiple stacks of paperwork on top of Daniel's desk in the left corner. Lynn walked out of the office and locked the outer office door after she placed the CLOSED sign in the window. Jessica sat down after she had poured herself a cup of coffee and put cream and sugar into it.

"Please tell me that you found something that will help my client with all of this paperwork," said Daniel, pointing at the stacks.

"I found plenty. First off, bronze is a copper alloy of sorts. I found out that Remington Ammunition Company manufacturers Bronze point® tipped, Core-lokt® bullets for a few, select rifle rounds," said Jessica.

"No handgun rounds?"

"Not specifically and I will go into detail about that later," she said in an as most determined voice she could find.

"Please continue," said Daniel as he started taking notes.

"The Bronze point®, Core-lokt® bullets are made primarily for big game hunting. They have been used by some law enforcement agencies for sniper use due to their extreme ballistic performance."

"Go on, you've got my attention," said Daniel.

"Taurus makes a solid copper bullet but in only one caliber. Winchester makes a solid copper bullet called an E-tip® round for rifle calibers only."

"What caliber is the Taurus round?"

". 45ACP. The bullet diameter is approximately .451 inches."

"Are any of the Remington rounds you found in the bullet diameter range?"

"None of the rounds are in that range."

"What else?"

"Winchester was asked by the U.S. Government to manufacture and test a shotgun round made of brass, another copper alloy, which was capable of penetrating armor plate up to .375 inches in thickness at a minimum of 10 yards. The round could also be used to blow a hole through a door that was suspected of being armor plated. Or, this round could blow the lock out of a door."

"So, we're talking a shotgun slug, then?"

"Yes, but there's more to it. These shotgun rounds, according to Winchester were .12-gauge, 2 ¾" shotgun shells made of brass and contained the brass sabot slug."

"Good Lord, when did Winchester manufacture this round?"

"From the spring of 1963 through the summer of 1970 when the government ordered Winchester to cease making the rounds for the Vietnam War."

"We will then assume that all stocks have been exhausted, right?"

"Yes," she said, handing Daniel all of the sheets off the top of one of the stacks. Jessica continued with her report as she prepared to hand more paperwork to Daniel.

"No handgun rounds were made of brass or other copper alloys with the exception of Taurus' copper bullets and only in one caliber. Remington currently manufactures the Bronze point®, Core-lokt® bullet in a few select rifle rounds. Now, Remington manufacturers a Brass Jacketed Hollow Point they call a Golden Saber™ round for handguns."

"Any of those rounds in the diameter range?"

"Three. The .45ACP at 185 grains, again at 230 grains and the .45ACP +P round at 185 grains."

"How do we know and how can I convince a jury that the .45ACP or .45ACP +P is in the range?"

"SAAMI told me, Daniel," replied Jessica, getting ready to hand some more paperwork to Daniel.

"Who's SAAMI?"

"SAAMI is the Sporting Arms and Ammunition Manufacturer's Institute. Here's the information I found on them. They have been around since the 1920's," she said, handing the stack to Daniel.

"Anything else of importance?"

"Yes. According to SAAMI, the .454 Casual handgun/rifle is capable of firing the .44 magnum, .44 special and .44 Russian rounds as well."

"Good information to know."

"Anything else for me?" asked Jessica.

"Find out how tall the hillside is, that my client was shooting into, without snow on top. Also, find out if you can see the windows that my client allegedly shot out from where he was standing."

"Okay. I'll see you sometime tomorrow, then," said Jessica as she left.

Daniel spent the next few hours writing on the reports that Jessica had given him. He looked up and saw that it was well after 7:00 pm.

He decided to call it a night. Daniel stood up, stretched and shut off all the lights in the office. He put on his heavy jacket and shut the main door to the office. He set the alarm, locked the door and waited for the alarm to set. When he heard the three, long, loud beeps, he knew the alarm was set.

He could see his breath in both the streetlights and the car headlights as he started walking down the road towards Silverton. He walked slowly at first, but as it got colder, he walked faster. He was walking at a pretty fast pace when one of the vehicles that went by him had a light bar on top of it like a police car. The vehicle turned around and drove up beside Daniel. The driver turned on the overhead lights and rolled the passenger's side, front window down. Daniel saw the Ironton Town Marshal shield on the sleeve of the jacket.

"Marshal Halverston, is that you?" asked Daniel.

"Sure is. Why don't you get into the car and I'll give you a ride home. It's kind of cold out there, isn't it?"

"Yes, it is a little cold out here and thank you, Marshal Halverston," said Daniel as he got into the vehicle.

Julie drove him to his house in Silverton. As he was getting out of the police car, Julie turned to him.

"Daniel, the San Juan County Coroner, as you suspected, pulled two .45ACP slugs out of the corpse you found. Jason decided that those slugs were probably from Kim's gun, so he didn't need a ballistics match up. The fingerprints belonged to a fellow by the name of William Georgeton."

"Thank you, Marshal Halverston," said Daniel as he shut the door and started walking up to his house.

"I smell a set-up," said Daniel to himself as he walked inside of his warm house.

CHAPTER 8

Daniel arrived at the office early once again. He disarmed the alarm and unlocked the door. He went inside and started a pot of coffee. Lynn showed up an hour or so later. She picked up the *Ironton Gazette* and tossed it onto her desktop. She turned on her computer and started to check phone messages. Daniel came out of his office and set down several stacks of paperwork on her desktop. Lynn looked up at Daniel and put the newspaper down that she had started to read.

"Please make copies of these defense exhibits and give them to Linda," he said.

"Okay."

Daniel caught a glimpse of the newspaper's headline: "Greenhorn Attorney to Defend Illegal!" Daniel read the article completely, twice, before becoming very angry at the sensationalism in the article itself. He noted the reporter's name and who was the editor-in-chief. Lynn was over at the copier when Daniel picked up the phone. He called the editor's desk and was put on hold. A few minutes later, the editor-in-chief came over the receiver.

"Yes, Mr. Marcos, what can I do for you? Care to comment on the headline in today's morning edition?" he asked.

"I am not a happy camper about your headline in the morning's edition of the newspaper."

"I'm sorry to hear that, Mr. Marcos. However, the First Amendment does protect us here at the paper."

"The First Amendment only protects you and your newspaper personnel if you don't stray into one of the six areas that is NOT protected by the First Amendment, as defined by the U.S. Supreme Court. You strayed into one of those unprotected areas."

"Okay, so what if this newspaper did stray, as you call it, into one of those areas? What are you going to do about it?"

"I'm going to own your newspaper by tomorrow evening. You had better prepare your final edition for evening delivery."

"We've been threatened before and nothing ever comes of it," he said as he started laughing.

"You laugh at me again and it will be the last thing you and your newspaper do, you pencil pushing SOB!" yelled Daniel as he slammed the phone down.

Lynn looked over at Daniel.

"Is everything alright, Daniel?" she asked, hesitantly.

"That newspaper editor and the paper are finished. When you get through making all those copies, there is some dictation that needs to be done."

Lynn spent the next few hours making copies and putting the originals into the case file. The door opened and Jessica came in around 10:45 am. She went directly into Daniel's inner office and closed the door. Daniel smiled and prepared to take notes.

"The hillside is 26 feet high without the current eight feet of snow on top," she said, handing her report to Daniel.

"Good; can you see the house, though?" asked Daniel as he took her report.

"Yes, but unless you're standing several hundred feet to the right of where our client was allegedly shooting, you can't see the windows that were shot out. The hillside only allows a view of the backside of the house," she said, handing Daniel the still shots from the video she had taken earlier.

Daniel looked over the shots and then set them down on his desktop. He picked them back up, looked them over again and then set them back down on the desktop as he stared at the ceiling. For Daniel, things were starting to come together. He returned his stare back to Jessica.

"Make sure that Lynn pays you up through today. Be on stand-by for Grand Junction in April."

"Sure; anything else?"

"Find my client's parents, but be discreet about it. I will need them as character reference for Juan's defense."

"Where do I start looking?"

"I might suggest talking nicely to Roberto to obtain that information."

"Okay."

Jessica left his office and received a check for her services. Lynn prepared to drive the box full of paperwork to Linda in Silverton. Lynn returned about lunchtime. Daniel had prepared his opening statements to the jury and the court. After he had Lynn type up the statements, he made some minor changes to them. He handed them back to Lynn to retype.

"Lynn, make hotel arrangements for myself, you, Jessica, Roberto, Juan and Juan's parents in Grand Junction for the week of April 11th through the 19th of 2011."

"Okay. You're bringing Juan's parents to the U.S.?"

"Yes."

Daniel was going over other cases when the phone rang. Lynn put the person on hold and stepped into Daniel's inner office.

"Yes?" asked Daniel.

"It's Linda, she's on Line 1 and she wants to discuss terms on case number 10CR545, *The People V. Harry Swatford*."

"Oh, that is very good for my client," said Daniel as he pushed the flashing light on the phone.

"Hello Linda, good to hear your voice," said Daniel as pleasantly as he could.

"I'll give your client, Harry Swatford, a Class 3 Misdemeanor, $250.00 fine, no jail time and the conviction disappears off his record in about two years provided that he doesn't get into anymore trouble."

"Accepted, I'll give him a call. Did you get my defense exhibits?"

"Sure did, just a few minutes ago. Might take me awhile to go through all of it though, you sent a copier paper box full of stuff over."

"I wanted to make sure that I had given you full disclosure of defense's information; anything else?"

"On case number 09CR121, *The People V. Lou Penn,* I'll drop the charges due to the inconsistencies with the witness statements."

"Thank you. I will call that client as well; good-bye."

"Good-bye."

Lynn stepped back into Daniel's office. He handed her the notes that he had taken.

"Call those clients, close out their files and send them their final bills," said Daniel.

"Okay."

Daniel started reviewing the case file of his current client, Juan Rivera. He was going over the witness statements and the client's statement once again. He set the client's statement down on his desktop. Daniel walked out into the outer office to get himself a cup of coffee. Lynn had just hung up the phone.

"We have reservations confirmed in Grand Junction at the Ramada® Inn off of Horizon Drive and I-70."

"Good."

"I also found out that our trial will be held in Courtroom L, which is on the top floor, south end of the building."

"Excellent. Have you heard from Jessica yet?"

"Yes. She said that the property above the alleged murder site is indeed owned by one Roy Georgeton. She also confirmed that he doesn't like visitors calling. She said she used the county assessor's office to find the information."

"Tell her good work. I'm going to go see Marshal Beckman. I'll have lunch while I am out and I'm taking my cell phone," said Daniel as he grabbed his heavy jacket and left the office.

A few minutes later, Daniel walked into the Ironton Town Marshal's office. Marshal Beckman looked up and smiled.

"Mr. Marcos, what can I do for you?" he asked.

"I need pictures, headshots only, of the corpse I found and one of Roy Georgeton."

"Why do you need them, counselor?"

"I have reasonable suspicion that my client will recognize one of them. It's for my client's defense, sir."

"You know, you defense lawyers are really weird. I'll print them up and have Marshal Halverston drop them by your office."

"Thank you, Marshal Beckman."

Daniel left the marshal's office and went to the local café. He returned to the office in the middle of the afternoon. When he walked into his office, Her Honor Krysta Johnson greeted him. She was holding a thick case file. Daniel motioned for her to follow him into his inner office. Krysta shut the door and sat in a chair that was directly in front of Daniel.

"The file is sealed because of an on-going internal affairs investigation of one of the INS/ICE agents involved with the case, by the name of Roy Georgeton. I can confirm that both the deceased's parents and your client's parents were among the 200 plus deportees. The list includes the 20 or so INS/ICE agents aboard that plane. I can also confirm that the plane crash was considered suspicious."

"Thank you, Your Honor."

"Well, I have to go. I have to prepare for court tomorrow morning."

"I understand."

A few minutes after Krysta had left, Marshal Halverston showed up with the photos that Daniel had asked for. Daniel had Lynn call Juan and Roberto to have them come into the office. When they arrived, Daniel showed them the photos. Juan recognized the photo of Roy Georgeton immediately.

"That man was the INS agent who arrested my parents," said Juan, using his left index finger to tap the picture.

"Thank you, Juan and Roberto, you can go now."

"Yes, sir," they said as they left.

After they had left, Daniel walked out into the outer office to see Lynn preparing to go home for the day.

"Lynn, when you get in tomorrow, call Jessica. Tell her I have something very important for her to do."

"Okay; good-night."

As Daniel was leaving his office, the evening edition of the local newspaper arrived. Daniel took it from the paper delivery person and opened it up. Daniel's paperwork, that he had faxed and mailed to the lawyer firm in Durango who represented the newspaper, had worked. The editor-in-chief had printed a full retraction statement along with several sentences that Daniel thoroughly enjoyed reading.

"A gag order has been issued by His Honor Judge Larry Bishop concerning the case of the suspected New Year's Eve killer. His Honor feels that the case will be lost to prejudice before the actual trial starts. Attorney Daniel Marcos, Esquire, cited clear violations of his client's 5th, 6th and 14th Amendment rights according to a copy of the affidavit attached to the gag order."

Daniel smiled and drove home to Silverton. He then called a friend of his in Grand Junction.

"Daniel, good to hear your voice. What can I do for you?" asked Glenn.

"Glenn, do you still work for the FAA?"

"Sure do, going on eight years now."

"How would I get a copy of a crash report on an American plane that crashed in Mexico City?"

"Mexican aviation authorities aren't usually very cooperative, but I'll do my best. What was the flight number?"

"I don't know. All I know is, the plane took off from Nogales, Arizona and crashed on takeoff in Mexico City. The flight was carrying deportees."

"You're not talking about that flight the INS chartered, are you?"

"I believe so. Get me all the information on that flight you can. I'll be in the Grand Junction area the week of April 11th through the 19th."

"Will do; good-bye."

The next day turned out to be a little more exciting than most. A U.S. Marshal, an FBI agent and an Internal Affairs agent for INS by the name of Bill Tolds, confronted Daniel, upon his arrival to his office. The men were polite, but firm on telling Daniel to lay off of Roy Georgeton. Daniel decided to challenge Bill.

"Why should I lay off of Mr. Georgeton? Has he done something wrong?" asked Daniel, already knowing at least one possible answer.

"He stole something from INS," replied Bill, flatly.

"A high-powered rifle, perhaps?" asked Daniel as he smiled.

"Perhaps. Just lay off of Mr. Georgeton, Mr. Marcos and have a nice day."

Lynn went to say something, but Daniel silenced her by raising his right index finger up to his lips. When all of the men had left, Daniel turned to her.

"Let's go into the basement to talk," said Daniel.

They went downstairs into the basement after Lynn had locked up the main office door and put the CLOSED sign in the window. Once they were both down in the basement, Daniel shut the door to the basement.

"Looks like you've stirred up a hornet's nest, Daniel," said Lynn.

"Those federal agents wouldn't have known what was going on unless they had monitored the fax machine or our telephones," said Daniel.

"That's illegal, isn't it, without a search warrant?"

"Not necessarily. The USA PATRIOT ACT III gives those federal agents the authority to monitor anyone they think is doing no good."

"Should we have our stuff checked out for 'bugs'?"

"Good idea, but go to Durango. Find a private investigator there who specializes, or has training, in counter-electronic surveillance equipment to check out our office. I'll pay the fee, whatever it is."

"Let me get going. Should I use the business credit card?"

"By all means and I'm going home right now. Call me with the results."

"Will do."

Lynn drove to Durango. She found a private investigator that followed her back to the office in Ironton. The private investigator conducted a thorough, electronic scan of the office. Although the instruments he used didn't detect any 'bugs' in the office area, they did find something else. One of the instruments detected the presence of a transmitter for a laser observation and recording device.

It was a small, black box attached to the lower, right corner of a window in Daniel's office. The window was located directly behind where Daniel sat. The private investigator removed the box and dropped it into a glass of water shorting it out. He looked around the office some more, finding one of those black boxes attached to the left window near where Lynn sat. He destroyed that one as well. He finished off his paperwork and handed the bill to Lynn.

"That will cost you $ 7,500.00 for counter-electronic surveillance device detection and device destruction," said the man, smiling.

"Do you take Visa®?" asked Lynn, looking at both of the black boxes in the same glass of water.

"Sure do."

Lynn handed the man the credit card. The man ran the credit card through his main office in Durango over the phone. He handed the credit card back to Lynn who had to sign the receipt.

The man left after writing down some more information off the Visa® card. Lynn then called Daniel. She read the report to Daniel who said he would see Lynn at the office the next morning. Daniel was getting ready for bed when his doorbell rang. He looked at his cell phone to see what time it was. The cell phone said it was 2045 hours.

He walked down the stairs from his study room to the front door. Daniel was still dressed in his workout attire from earlier in the evening.

The black tank top, outlined in gold, accented his coal black hair and high cheek bones as well as showing off the rest of his Native American slightly tanned features; his muscular chest and arms. The shorts were black, outlined in orange showing off his muscular and slightly tanned legs. He opened the door to find a woman standing there on the porch. She took one look at his body and almost fainted.

"Yes, madam, what can I do for you?" Daniel asked, pleasantly.

"I'm Mary Jean, the reporter from the *Ironton Gazette* who wrote the article that nearly got the newspaper shutdown today," she said, nicely.

"Well Mary, do you have your press credentials?" asked Daniel, unfazed by her opening remark.

"Yes I do, right here, chesty," she said, opening up the folding leather wallet with her picture and press identification. Daniel looked it over.

"Why don't you come inside? Would you like some tea?" he asked.

"Yes, I would love to come inside and I would love to be in court with you, Mr. Marcos," she said, stumbling over her own words.

Daniel used his left hand to shut the door as he used his right hand to point to a chair to the right of the door. He poured them both a cup of tea. She gave Daniel another look-over before taking a sip of the tea. She could taste lemon and orange spices immediately with a dash of cinnamon. Mary set her cup of tea down on the small tabletop that was directly in front of her. She then took out her small notepad from her purse and grabbed a pen from her upper right, jacket pocket.

"Are you going to interview me?" asked Daniel.

"Yes, that was my intention; sex afterwards?" she asked, accidentally.

"I hate reporters," replied Daniel in a flat tone of voice.

"Why?"

"No reporter nor newspaper since the beginning of the 20th Century has been able to sell any newspapers printing the truth. The truth is dull and boring. The only thing that seems to sell any newspapers, newsprint or airtime is sensationalism and innuendos. Do I make myself clear?"

"Very clear, chesty. I promise that this interview will be published word for word exactly as you answered the questions."

"Since there is only a verbal agreement between you and I, I'll have to trust you. However, make one mistake and I will own that newspaper in 24 hours. I don't make idle threats."

"The gag order was very clear on that issue."

"What's on your mind?"

The interview continued until around 2315 hours. Mary had finished off her tea and Daniel was tired. He let her out the door and then went to bed. He could hardly wait to read the next morning's edition of the local newspaper.

The next morning, Daniel met Lynn at the office. He had Lynn call Jessica telling her what to look for. She looked around her office windows and found one of the black boxes, which she smashed with a hammer. After the thing was destroyed, the fax machine came to life.

She took the pages off the fax machine. The pages contained the admission and discharge paperwork for Juan's parents. Juan's parents had been in the hospital for three weeks. When they were discharged, an unknown person picked them up and took them back to the Mexico City airport. There, they were put on another plane and flown to the capital city of Honduras. After they stepped off the plane in the capital city of Honduras, they returned to their village. The name of the village was almost unpronounceable.

Jessica jumped onto her computer and typed in the name of the village into MapQuest®. MapQuest® said that the name provided matched a village lying some 100km to the west of the capital city of Honduras. The roads weren't marked in a normal fashion. The road to the village was simply labeled HON-17A.

She called Daniel and relayed the information to him. He was pleased with the breakthrough in the case and he told her to come in to see him. Jessica showed up about half an hour later.

"Make sure that Lynn pays you up-to-date for your time. Go to Honduras; find my client's parents. Take along those pictures of William and Roy Georgeton to see if anyone recognizes either of them."

"Will do, but I don't have all of my shots up-to-date yet. I still need five more shots before traveling to Mexico or Honduras."

"When will you be done with them?"

"April 9th."

"Make reservations to fly to Honduras from Denver. Take the business credit card with you and call me on my personal cell phone, not the business cell phone, with any developments."

"Will do."

Time was running out for Juan and the others involved. Daniel was convinced that her office getting trashed, the corpse, the aircraft crash and all the 'bugs' were all connected somehow. Daniel went to and from work as usual. Two days before Daniel had to leave, Glenn called him.

"Daniel, this is Glenn. I wasn't able to get a copy of the crash report, but I did get the name of the crash investigator."

"Who was it?"

"Julio Juarez. He works at the Mexico City Airport in the office of the Mexican version of the FAA. I'm not very familiar with them."

"Thanks, Glenn," said Daniel, hanging up the phone. He turned around and called Jessica.

"Jessica, could you please make a stop in Mexico City and talk to a Julio Juarez? He works in the Mexican version of the FAA."

"Sure, but that means I will have to fly out of DIA instead of Durango."

"Take along plenty of cash and don't forget to call."

"Sure."

Daniel drove Jessica to DIA from Grand Junction. Jessica boarded a plane for Mexico City with a final destination of the capital city of Honduras. She clutched her passport tightly as the plane took off. Buried in her luggage, unknown to her at the time, were two subpoenas in Spanish ordering Juan's parents to appear in court. Daniel hoped that the subpoenas would be enough to get Juan's parents into the country through customs.

CHAPTER 9

When Jessica took off from Denver, Colorado, it was ten degrees below zero without wind-chill. There was blowing snow and the plane had to be de-iced before takeoff. When she landed in Mexico City, it was nighttime and the temperature was 80 degrees with a slight wind blowing in from the west. As she stepped off the plane, she was already starting to sweat in the turtleneck shirt and long pants she was wearing when she had left Denver. She checked through customs and went to the baggage claim area. She picked up her bags and her rental car.

She drove to the hotel and checked into her room. Next, after finding out that Mexico City was on Central Standard Time, she called Daniel. Daniel had told her to call him with any developments on his private cell phone. He further instructed her to call him collect if necessary. She decided that tomorrow, she would go see the Transportation Department and find Julio Juarez. She went to sleep after taking a shower.

The next day turned out to be Saturday. That meant the government offices were closed until Monday morning. Jessica decided to go to the hospital first. She ended up driving around in multiple circles before finding the hospital. She parked the car and walked into the front entrance. Jessica found the check-in/information desk that was manned by two nurses; she approached the desk.

Speaking Spanish, she asked where the nurse was working that was listed on the discharge paperwork. One of the nurses at the check-in/information desk told Jessica to check the eighth floor. Jessica went to the eighth floor and found the nurse. They went into a small break room on the floor.

"Do you remember a plane crash that happened about six or seven years ago?" asked Jessica, in Spanish, as she pulled out a notepad and pen from her purse.

"Yes, I do. What a terrible tragedy. 22 survivors out of the 230 people aboard," the nurse responded in good English like it was just yesterday.

"You speak good English, Nurse Calixip," replied Jessica in English.

"We get a lot of foreigners down here. It helps to speak their language."

"You're right. Do you remember these people being in your ward up here?" asked Jessica, showing the nurse the paperwork.

"Oh, yes. A man, with severely broken legs and a woman with badly broken arms. Our orthopedic surgeons did the best they could with the equipment they had available to them. I am certain that your country's orthopedic surgeons could have done a much better repair job. You know they were being sent back to Honduras by your government, right?"

"Yes, they were. Do you recognize either of these two men as the one who picked them up when they were discharged?" asked Jessica who had put up the paperwork and pulled out the pictures of Roy Georgeton and William Georgeton. She showed them to the nurse.

"It was this man right here," she said, using her left index finger to point at William Georgeton.

"Thank you and you've been most helpful," said Jessica, giving the woman some money.

"Why, thank you, my dear. Any particular reason for the donation to the hospital?" the nurse asked, taking the money.

"A donation to the hospital to get better equipment in the name of Attorney Daniel Marcos, Esquire."

"Any time, my dear," she replied, putting the money into her left, front pants pocket.

Jessica left and returned to her hotel. She called Daniel with the information.

"Great work, Jessica. Did you get a receipt for the donation you made in my name?"

"No, I didn't know that I needed to have a receipt."

"It was for income tax purposes; don't worry about it. Keep up the diligent work; goodbye."

Now all she had to do was wait until Monday to try and find one Julio Juarez. She slept as much as she could until Monday morning. Now, it was off to find Julio Juarez, if he really existed at all.

Daniel, Lynn, Juan and Roberto all drove in the same car to the Mesa County Courthouse. Reporters from a few of the newspapers around Colorado met them. This included Mary from the *Ironton Gazette.*

This caused Daniel, Lynn, Roberto and Juan to have to push their way through. After passing through security, they walked into courtroom L. Daniel and Lynn could see the bailiff. Juan took his seat to the left of Daniel as Lynn took a seat to the far left of Daniel on the end of the table. The bailiff stood at attention when the judge entered the courtroom.

"All rise, Courtroom L of the Mesa County Courthouse is now in session. The Honorable Judge Larry Bishop, presiding, in the case of *The People v. Juan Rivera,* case number 11CR1," said Sergio.

"You may be seated," said Larry as he sat down in the chair behind the bench.

"Your Honor, defense counsel would like to approach the bench," said Daniel.

"Does the prosecution have a problem with defense counsel's request?" asked Larry.

"No objections, Your Honor, as long as I am present for this conversation."

"Defense counsel?"

"No problems, Your Honor."

Both Linda and Daniel walked up to the bench.

"Your Honor, since it is too late to get the charges dropped against my client, I would like to have a recess called when my private cell phone rings," said Daniel.

"This is highly irregular, counselor. Does the prosecution have a problem with the request?"

"None, Your Honor."

"Why do you need access to your cell phone on such short notice, counselor?" asked Larry, while Linda watched intently.

"I am aware that my request is highly irregular, Your Honor. I maintain that my client is innocent and I am awaiting confirmation of a big piece of vital evidence at this time on the way to proving my client's innocence."

"Where is this piece of vital evidence coming from?" asked Linda.

"From Honduras, counselor," said Daniel.

"I have no objections, Your Honor, provided that I get a copy of any evidence that defense counsel may obtain," said Linda.

"Do you have any objections to the prosecution's request, counselor?" asked Larry.

"None, Your Honor. I'm only interested in the truth. I hope that The People are as interested in the truth as I am?" asked Daniel, looking at Linda.

"The People are interested in the truth, very well," replied Larry on Linda's behalf.

"Ladies and Gentlemen of the jury, this is the trial phase of the *People V. Juan Rivera III,* case number 11CR1. A prospective jury has been summoned for this case and has been seated in the jury box. There are twelve prospective jurors being nine primary and three alternates," said Larry as everyone sat down.

Larry put on his reading glasses and opened the case file that was sitting before him on his left. He briefly glanced over to his right to see the whiteboard before continuing his speech.

"Are there any members of the jury that do not reside in Mesa County?" asked Larry as he looked over at the jury box; four hands went up, so he stopped the rest of his speech. He looked down at the whiteboard that had been placed in front of him by the main jury coordinator for Mesa County. Her assistant jury coordinator was in the courtroom with Larry, standing to the left of his bench.

"Juror number twenty, seated in primary spot four, where do you reside, sir?" asked Larry

"I reside, at this time, in Baca County."

"Very well, sir, you are dismissed. Please see the main jury coordinator on the first floor. Assistant jury coordinator; please call another juror to replace them."

"Yes, Your Honor; juror number sixty-two, please take their place," he said.

Juror number sixty-two took their place in primary jury box number four.

"Madam, do you reside in Mesa County?" asked Larry.

"Yes, Your Honor, I do," she said smiling.

"Thank you," replied Larry, going on to the next raised hand. That person was seated in primary jury box number six.

"Juror number fifteen, seated in primary spot six, where do you currently reside, madam?" asked Larry.

"I currently live in the State of Utah, Your Honor," she said.

"Very well, you're dismissed. Please see the main jury coordinator on the first floor. Assistant jury coordinator; please call another juror to replace them."

"Yes, Your Honor; juror number one hundred eighteen, please take their place."

Juror number one hundred eighteen took their place.

"Do you, sir, reside in Mesa County?"

"I do, Your Honor."

Larry looked down at the whiteboard to see where the other two hands were located. He went to alternate juror number one first.

"Juror number fifty, where do you currently reside, sir?"

"In Denver County, Your Honor."

"Very well, you are dismissed. Please see the main jury coordinator on the first floor. Assistant jury coordinator; please call another juror to replace them."

"Yes, Your Honor; juror number seventy-three, take their place."

Juror number seventy-three took their place.

"Do you, madam, reside in Mesa County?"

"I do, Your Honor."

Larry went to the last raised hand.

"Juror number ninety, where do you currently reside, sir?"

"Montezuma County, Your Honor."

"Very well, you're dismissed. Please see the main jury coordinator on the first floor. Assistant jury coordinator, please call another juror."

"Yes, Your Honor; juror number one hundred forty-two, take their place."

Juror number one hundred forty-two took their place.

"Do you, madam, reside in Mesa County?"

"I do, Your Honor."

Larry paused for a few minutes before he started his speech back up again.

"Are there any members of the jury that are not 18 years of age?"

One hand went up, so he looked down to see that it was juror number fifty-eight in primary juror position eight.

"Yes, primary juror number eight, how old are you?" asked Larry as he looked at him.

"I'm seventeen, Your Honor."

"Very well, you're dismissed. Please see the main jury coordinator on the first floor. Assistant jury coordinator, please call another juror to replace them."

"Yes, Your Honor; juror number eighty, take their place."

Juror number eighty took their place.

"Juror number eighty, I surmise that you are over eighteen?"

"I am, Your Honor. I am forty-four."

Larry paused once again before continuing.

"Are there any members of the jury that cannot see or hear well enough to be a juror?"

No hands went up, so Larry continued with his speech.

"Are there any members of the jury that cannot read, speak or write English?"

One hand went up; it was juror number thirty-six seated in alternate juror two's position. Larry looked at the man for a few seconds before he concluded that the man was of Asian descent.

"Juror number thirty-six seated in alternate juror two's position, you cannot speak, read or write English?" asked Larry.

The man shook his head in a negative fashion.

"Very well, you're dismissed. Please see the main jury coordinator on the first floor. Assistant jury coordinator, call another juror to replace them."

The man stood up and started looking around the courtroom in a confused manner before the bailiff started pointing towards the exit of the courtroom. The man almost ran to the exit.

"Yes, Your Honor; juror number one hundred ninety-nine, take their place."

Juror number one hundred ninety-nine took their place.

"I surmise, sir that you can speak, read and write English?"

"Yes, Your Honor I can. I can also speak, read and write Arabic, Korean, Klingon and Romulan."

"That's very impressive, sir; thank you for being so truthful in this matter," replied Larry before continuing.

"Are there any members of the jury that have had prior jury duty service, meaning that you were selected as a juror for a criminal or civil trial in the past twelve months?"

One hand went up from juror number twenty-nine.

"Sir, you are primary juror number nine in the front row. When was your jury service?"

"Four months ago in a civil trial in this very courtroom, Your Honor," he said standing up.

"Very well, you're dismissed. Please see the main jury coordinator on the first floor. Assistant jury coordinator, call another juror to replace them."

"Yes, Your Honor; juror number four hundred, take their place."

Juror number four hundred took their place.

"Do you have any prior jury duty service, madam?"

"No, Your Honor; the last time I was called for jury duty was eleven years ago."

Larry could tell this was going to be a long day for him and everyone else in the jury pool. Since it was almost lunchtime, Larry dismissed everyone for lunch. When everyone had returned from lunch, Larry started the questioning of the jurors once again.

"Are there any members of the jury that know any members of the parties or witnesses involved in this case?"

No hands went up, so Larry continued with his speech.

"Are there any members of the jury that know anything about this case from radio, TV, Internet or newspapers?"

One hand went up from the front row of primary jurors. Juror number sixty, who was in juror number one's position raised their hand.

"Sir, what do you know about this case?"

"I had read a newspaper article a few days ago that the defendant is possibly an illegal alien in this country. I hate illegal aliens, Your Honor," he said, loudly.

"Prosecution, do you have a problem with this prospective juror?" asked Larry.

"Yes, Your Honor, the State does have a slight problem with the prospective juror; release for voir dire, Your Honor," said Linda as she stood up and then sat back down.

"Very well, sir, you're dismissed. Please see the main jury coordinator on the first floor. Assistant jury coordinator, call another juror to replace them."

"Yes, Your Honor; juror number three hundred, take their place."

Juror number three hundred took their place. The jurors moved around for the last time before Larry prepared to let the other prospective jurors go. He looked over his whiteboard one more time before he looked at the spectator's area at the other prospective alternate jurors.

"Thank you all for showing up today for possible jury selection and jury service. I do apologize for any inconvenience that this process may have caused you. You are now free to go. Please see the main jury coordinator on the first floor before you leave."

Larry turned the courtroom over to the prosecution first. Daniel was going over some notes that he had been taking during the jury selection process. Linda stood up to address the court.

"Your Honor, the prosecution is satisfied with the jury that has been selected," she said as she sat back down.

"So noted that the prosecution is satisfied with the jury selected; is defense counsel satisfied with the jury selected?"

"That will be contingent on the answer I receive from the jury to a couple of questions," said Daniel as he stood up.

"Does the prosecution have any objections to defense counsel's questions to the jury?"

"None, Your Honor," she said standing up and then sitting back down.

"Go ahead and ask your question."

"Ladies and gentlemen of the jury and jury alternates, do you believe that everyone is innocent until proven guilty?"

The jurors all shook their heads up and down.

"Do you believe that the accused here, my client, should receive a fair trial based upon the fact that he is entitled to such amenities under the letter of the law?"

The jurors all shook their heads up and down again.

"Thank you, ladies and gentlemen of the jury. I am satisfied with the jury, Your Honor."

Daniel and Linda returned to their seats. The jury box was filled with the first twelve potential jurors. Thankfully, by the end of the day, the nine primary jurors had been selected along with three alternates. The jury consisted of two Native American males about Juan's age. There were two female Hispanics about Juan's age and two African-Americans, one male and one female. There were two more females, both Caucasians and one male Eskimo. The three alternates were all black males. The judge decided to call it a day and ordered that the trial would reconvene the next morning.

Jessica had spent the day looking for Julio. She finally found him at an abandoned hangar on the airport's property. After she had paid him some $2,000.00 U.S. Dollars for the information she wanted, Julio took her into his office. There, he opened up a filing cabinet. The filing cabinet contained all the photos, reports and notes on the crash.

"Please take anything you like back to your hotel room tonight and look at it. In the morning, I will take you out into the desert where the pieces are at," said Julio.

"Thank you, Julio," said Jessica, rather suspicious of his sudden cooperation.

Jessica went back to her hotel room to find it had been trashed. After she cleaned up the mess, the only thing missing was her plane ticket to the capital city of Honduras; Tegucigalpa. She called Daniel and told him what had happened.

"Jessica, be really careful down there. Your room getting trashed wasn't a random thing and neither was this random taking of your airline ticket. Get another airline ticket. The real killer framed my client and I suspect one of his or her representatives is down there with you."

"Will do. Tomorrow Julio, if it really is him, is taking me out into the desert to where the pieces of the aircraft are located."

"Be careful and don't miss even the smallest detail; it could be vital."

"Will do," she said, hanging up the phone. Jessica then ordered, from the room service menu, the biggest bottle of the best Tequila made. She had it charged to the room knowing that she might need it to smooth things over with someone.

The next morning Julio picked up Jessica at her hotel. She tossed the bottle of alcohol into the backseat as they took off into the desert in a small, foreign made sports car that didn't have any seatbelts in it. Julio was driving like a banshee to the area at speeds over 140 KMH on the speedometer. When they arrived at the aircraft graveyard, Julio tried to take Jessica in to where all the pieces were located.

The guard at the entrance refused to allow Julio, despite his credentials, nor Jessica into the aircraft junkyard. Julio argued with the guard. Next, he tried to bribe the man, when that didn't work, he returned to the car in defeat.

"I am sorry, Seniorita Kim. The guard says he is under orders not to let anyone in today," said Julio.

"May I try to get us inside?" asked Jessica.

"Be my guest," replied Julio as he wondered what Jessica was doing in the backseat.

Jessica exited the vehicle with both money, in the form of $20.00 bills, and the bottle of alcohol. She entered the guard shack as the guard looked up at her. Speaking in Spanish, they conversed.

"I really, really, really need to get into the junkyard to see the wreckage of that plane."

"Not possible, Seniorita Kim," he said, flatly.

"Please," she replied, setting the bottle of alcohol down on the desktop.

The guard looked over the bottle carefully and then put it into the bottom, right hand drawer of the desk. Next, Jessica started dropping $20.00 bills on the desktop until there was $500.00 U.S. dollars sitting on the desktop. The guard opened the gate and they drove to the wreckage. Jessica took in the sight of all the pieces.

She walked through a forest of twisted hunks of metal that had once been the fuselage section of the Fokker F-28, Executive Jet. She carefully walked around piles of other debris and finally found what she was looking for, the tail section. The tail section was where Juan's parents had been. The rest of the plane had been blackened by the fire and resultant explosion.

Jessica looked over the landing gear pieces. She found where a piece of the left landing gear strut had broken off and had been hurled into the fuel tanks under the left wing. Jessica began developing a gruesome picture in her mind of the mayhem and carnage that had occurred.

She bent down and looked over the landing gear strut and tire. The sidewall of the tire had been blown out. According to the investigation notes that she had read the night before, the plane was going about 250 KMH when the accident happened. She put on a pair of thick, leather gloves and started looking around the inside of where the gash in the tire was located.

Her right index finger hit something hard on the inside of the rim. She then used her left hand to tear the hole open wider. Something inside was shining back at her in the desert sunlight. She turned to Julio.

"Do you have a pair of pliers, tongs, anything like that and a plastic bag?" she asked him in Spanish.

"Yes," he replied.

Julio ran off and returned later with a plastic sandwich baggie and a pair of slightly rusted, long needle nose pliers. He handed the items to Jessica.

"Did you find something that the investigators missed, seniorita?" asked Julio excitedly.

"I believe so," she replied in Spanish as she carefully removed a shiny piece of bullet fragment. The bullet fragment had a piece of bronze attached to the front of it. Jessica dropped the bullet fragment into the plastic bag and put the bag into her right, front pants pocket.

"Was that a piece of a bullet?" asked Julio, grinning.

"I believe so. But a crime lab is the only one who could tell positively."

"My cousin works for the Mexico City Police Department, can he do whatever it is that needs to be done?"

"Sure. Let's go see your cousin."

Another dreadfully fast trip across the desert forced Jessica into leaving claw marks on the passenger's seat and dashboard. Julio took the bullet fragment into the police station. Jessica decided it was time for another $1,000.00 cash for insurance purposes, so she gave it to Julio to give to his cousin as a thank you for checking on the piece of possible bullet.

A few minutes later, Julio and Julio's cousin came out into the waiting room. They were both very excited and despite a cash donation to the desk sergeant, Jessica wasn't allowed back to the crime lab. Julio's cousin finally said something to the desk sergeant who begrudgingly let her back into the crime lab.

"The bullet fragment you gave my cousin, Julio, here, more than likely came from a high-powered rifle."

"Is it possible that piece of stuff I gave you is from the plane?" she asked.

"No, Seniorita Kim, that is not part of the plane. There is a slim possibility that the bullet could have come from a single shot handgun chambered to fire this particular rifle caliber," said Julio's cousin.

"Can you tell me what caliber?" asked Jessica, ready to take notes as she withdrew a pen and notepad from her purse once again.

"Assuming that the piece you gave me is one-quarter of the full size of the bullet, the caliber is closest to 7MM Magnum, 7MM-08 or .284 Winchester. I measured the bullet base diameter to be about .284 inches."

"Could you hit a fast moving target with a bolt-action rifle?"

"No, Seniorita, in order to hit a target moving at, say, about 250 KMH, the rifle would have to be a semi-automatic."

"Do you know of any civilian or military semi-automatic rifles that can fire any of those rounds you mentioned?"

"Only one that I can think of; Remington Firearms manufactures a semi-automatic hunting rifle chambered to fire the 7mm-08 round."

"Thank you, you've been most helpful."

"Anytime," he replied, taking another $500.00 from Jessica.

As soon as Jessica returned to her hotel room, she packed up. She then drove to the airport. There she turned in the rental car and pulled more cash from an ATM machine. She then purchased another ticket to Tegucigalpa. While at the airport, waiting for her flight, she called Daniel.

Daniel was listening to the DA's opening statements. She thundered away at the jury about how coldblooded the defendant was, among other things. When she had finished her opening statements, even Daniel was a little scared. He stood up to give his opening statement and noticed his private cell phone was flashing.

"Your Honor, my cell phone is ringing," said Daniel answering it as he left the courtroom to go outside into the hallway.

"Ten minute recess," said Larry, banging his gavel down and rolling his eyes.

Out in the hallway, Daniel was getting excited about the news Jessica was giving him. As he hung up his cell phone and prepared to go back into the courtroom, Glenn showed up. Daniel looked up and they hugged briefly.

"Glenn, it's good to see you," said Daniel.

"It's good to see you as well. I had today off, so I thought I might join the spectators."

"It's good to have a friend here. By the way, how many people were aboard that flight when it crashed?"

"I thought you might ask that question. I finally got the crash report and it's sitting on my desk at Walker Field. The report listed 230 deportees aboard that flight including 12 INS/ICE agents. There were 22 deportee survivors."

"That crash was no accident, Glenn. How soon before you can get down there with a proper team of crash inspectors?"

"I suppose you have evidence to back up this trip to Mexico City."

"That plane was a Fokker F-28, Executive Jet wasn't it?"

"Yes."

"The left tire and strut were shot out by someone using a semi-automatic rifle chambered either in 7MM magnum, 7MM-08 or .284 Winchester. My private investigator down there just received the ballistics report from the partial bullet fragment she dug out of the tire."

"I'll see what I can do."

Lynn came out into the hallway.

"Please ask for five more minutes," said Daniel.

"I'll try," she said going back into the courtroom.

"Glenn, think about this angle. All 12 INS/ICE agents killed in that crash, I suspect, had a $250,000.00 life insurance policy. I think you will find that there is probably an addendum to that life insurance policy, called a rider, for an additional $50,000.00 if the person is killed in the line of duty."

"So you think this is some sort of insurance money scam?"

"Yes. I will bet you no complete bodies were ever recovered from that crash site, were there?"

"True, only the 22 survivors in the tail section were rescued."

"Something tells me that of those survivors, only my client's parents and the deceased parents had any children."

"I'll find out for you and let you know; anything else?"

"Yeah. If you and your team do get to the Mexico City Airport, I'll bet you find either the shell casings or the magazine from the weapon in question. I promise that if you find either one, I'll get you the rifle that fired those rounds."

"I'm on my way."

Daniel walked back into the courtroom and approached the jury box. He smiled and looked at all the jurors in their eyes.

"After that scary opening statement by my esteemed colleague, I was ready to run away." Daniel smiled again as the jurors chuckled a little.

"My client didn't kill those people because I will not defend a client who is guilty. By the end of this trial, the real killer will be exposed; thank you," said Daniel as he watched the jurors reactions to his simple statement while he sat down. The jurors had responded to Daniel favorably.

"Very well, defense counsel. The prosecution, if ready, may call its first witness," said Larry.

"The People call Nabiya Quartez to the stand," said Linda.

Nabiya walked passed Linda and took the seat in the witness stand. Sergio swore her in and she sat down.

"Will you please tell the court your name and occupation," said Linda.

"My name is Nabiya Quartez and I am the San Juan County Coroner in the State of Colorado."

"How long have you served in that position?"

"Since my appointment by the San Juan county commissioners about 12 years ago. I also hold a degree in pathology from Iowa State University since 1990. I also served as the Medical Examiner for Prowers County, Colorado, from 1988 to 1990 and I served as the assistant Boulder County, Colorado, Coroner from 1992 to 1996."

"I'm impressed, Miss Quartez," said Daniel.

"Why, thank you, counselor," she replied.

"Did you, on the morning of the 1st of January of this year, have the duty to determine how two people had died?" asked Linda as she walked over to the evidence table to pick up several pieces of paperwork to give to Nabiya.

"Yes. There were two bodies in my morgue awaiting an after-death examination commonly known in my profession as a post mortem," responded Nabiya, taking the paperwork.

"Is that your coroner's report and signatures on those death certificates?" asked Linda.

Nabiya looked over the paperwork.

"Yes, that is my coroner's report, known as the post mortem. That is also my signature on the police report and statements as well as the death certificates," she said, shuffling through the paperwork.

"Would you read to the court the manner of death of the two people," said Linda as she looked at Daniel.

Nabiya put on her reading glasses and looked over her initial report. She cleared her throat before speaking.

"Removed two badly damaged bullets and a third partial bullet fragment. Bullet number one was removed from the Hispanic male infant's skull just above the right eye. Bullet number two was removed from the right lung of the Hispanic female. The partial bullet fragment was removed from the left ribcage of the Hispanic female."

"Please go on," said Linda.

"Bullet number one penetrated the left shoulder and sliced through the aorta artery before exiting just above the left breast. There it entered the infant's skull, causing massive bleeding in the brain which resulted in death."

"Thank you, no further questions, Your Honor," said Linda.

"Does the defense counsel wish to cross-exam?" asked Larry after a few minutes of seeing Daniel stare at the wall behind Larry.

"Yes, Your Honor. Miss Quartez, would you please tell me which bullet was fatal to both parties?" asked Daniel.

"Bullet number one, which had sliced through the aorta and then entered the infant's brain."

"What about bullet number two?"

"Bullet number two could only have been fatal to the female since it totally collapsed the right lung."

"Did you notice any other marks on the female Hispanic's body?"

"Yes. There was what appeared to be a puncture mark on the female's right arm."

"Objection, Your Honor, irrelevant and immaterial; calls for an opinion of the witness. Where is defense counsel going with this line of questioning?" asked Linda.

"I propose, Your Honor, that the third bullet entered the female's body and left behind a piece of itself in her left ribcage. It was this bullet and the person who fired it, that is critical to my client's defense," said Daniel.

"Objection overruled. The witness will answer the question," said Larry.

"Yes, Mr. Marcos, I did remove a piece of unknown material, which turned out to be a bullet fragment, from the female's left ribcage."

"Could you tell this court if that piece of bullet fragment you removed had contact with either bullets you removed?"

"No, I cannot tell you if that piece of bullet fragment had contact with either bullet."

"So, it is possible that piece of metal may have sliced through the aorta and the other bullets were thrown in for good measure by the real killer and that piece of bullet is what caused death?" asked Daniel as he faced the jury box.

"Yes, it is possible."

"No further questions, Your Honor," said Daniel.

"Any recross, prosecution?" asked Larry.

"No, Your Honor," replied Linda.

"The witness is excused. This court is recessed until tomorrow morning at 8:00 am," said Larry, banging his gavel down.

CHAPTER 10

The plane landed in Tegucigalpa, Honduras, a little past 1:00 pm local time. She looked up at one of the many welcoming boards on the concourse she had entered to check the time before looking at her watch. She looked at her watch and the time matched. This told Jessica that Honduras and Grand Junction, Colorado were in the same time zone. Jessica went through customs for the country of Honduras and rented a car. She then drove to a local hotel and checked in.

She was a little upset that MapQuest® had been wrong in the road directions. The village she needed was actually 120 KM to the east. The heat and humidity were stifling for her. She turned on the hotel room's air conditioning system.

The air temperature was 87 degrees and the relative humidity level was approximately 98%. This gave a heat index, as she saw on the local weather station she tuned into in the hotel room, of 115 degrees. Soon, she was soaked in sweat despite the air conditioning in the room. She planned on getting up early the next morning to drive to the village.

Daniel, Lynn, Juan and Roberto were getting out of Daniel's car when Glenn came running over to them. Glenn had some paperwork with him. Daniel motioned for Lynn, Juan and Roberto to go inside the courthouse. They took the elevator to the third floor and walked into courtroom L. Daniel looked at Glenn as Glenn handed Daniel the paperwork.

"You were right about the life insurance policy angle. Eight of the agents killed were married with no children. The other four had only ailing relatives who have since passed away."

"Good work, Glenn. What about the survivors?"

"You were right about that angle as well. Only your client and the deceased were children survivors. None of the other deportees appeared to have any close, living relatives."

"I really smell a set-up now; anything else?"

"Not yet."

"Stay on it and be very careful. The killer could have some 'moles' lying in wait for someone like you and your team. The killer or his or her friends may be willing to kill again to cover up their tracks."

"I'll be very careful."

Daniel entered the courtroom, set the paperwork down on the desktop before sitting down in the chair. Lynn looked at him suspiciously before the judge scolded him.

"I do hope defense counsel has a good reason for being late. I was about to find you in contempt of court," said Larry, sternly.

"I do, Your Honor. I would like this paperwork to be entered into evidence as defense exhibits E1 through E4. If my esteemed colleague would like to have copies of this paperwork, I have no objections," said Daniel, holding up the paperwork.

"Bailiff, please get the papers," said Larry.

Sergio obtained the papers and handed them to Larry. Larry looked them over and handed them back to Sergio. Sergio took the papers over to Linda. Linda took the papers and sent her legal assistant to make copies.

"Your Honor, I have no objections to the prosecution calling its next witness, pending either a phone call or a possible fax," said Daniel.

"So noted. The People may call their next witness," said Larry.

"The People call Garth Smith to the stand," said Linda.

Garth stood up from the spectator's area and took the stand. He was sworn in and after he had sat down, Linda approached him.

"Mr. Smith, on the morning of January 3rd of this year, did you do a ballistics check on this item labeled prosecution exhibit 4?" she asked, handing Mr. Smith the revolver.

"Yes, I did," he replied, looking at the weapon.

"How do you know that this is the revolver you tested?"

"Simple, the serial number matches the serial number in my ballistics report. Also, I put a piece of blue tape, from the ballistics lab, over the top of the hammer with my initials on it."

"Did you find the defendant's fingerprints on the weapon during your check?" asked Linda.

"Objection, Your Honor; irrelevant and immaterial. Of course my client's fingerprints are going to be on the weapon; he owns it," said Daniel.

Linda put the revolver back down on the evidence table. She then picked up the ballistics report, handing it to Garth.

"Objection sustained," said Larry.

Daniel leaned over to Juan and whispered something into his right ear.

"Did you use up all the ammunition you bought for the gun the night you were arrested?"

"Yes. The box only contained 20 rounds."

"Good," said Daniel as he returned his attention to Linda's line of questioning.

"Calling your attention to prosecution exhibit 5, your ballistics report. Did you find the deceased's blood on the bullets you received from the San Juan County Coroner?"

"Yes, I did. The blood typing and tissue-matching test came back positive for the deceased. The deceased was a rare blood type AB negative as was her infant son."

"Thank you. No further questions," said Linda.

Daniel stood up and took the ballistics report from Linda and gave the report back to Garth.

"Mr. Smith, would you please read to the court, the comments field of your report?" asked Daniel.

"Objection, Your Honor. The comments field of the report has no direct bearing on this case," said Linda.

"Your Honor, the comments field is yet another part of the client's defense," replied Daniel quickly.

"Objection overruled. The witness will answer the question," said Larry

"Sure," he said, clearing his throat before continuing.

"Bullets were too badly damaged; unable to completely match up bullets to weapon provided for testing. Bullet diameters are from .429 inches in diameter to .456 inches in diameter. Piece of metal submitted in evidence bag with bullets tested positive for bronze and does not match any known handgun bullets."

"Thank you, Mr. Smith. Mr. Smith, would you read paragraph six of your report," asked Daniel.

"Objection, Your Honor, irrelevant and immaterial. Calls for facts not already entered into evidence," said Linda.

"Your Honor, it is that paragraph which contains a vital piece of evidence for my client's defense. I ask for the facts to be entered into evidence for the defense," said Daniel as he picked up two evidence bags from the evidence table. He handed the bags to Garth.

"Objection overruled. Defense counsel, you need to be a bit more careful next time."

"I will, Your Honor and thank you. Mr. Smith, would you please explain, for the jury's and the court's enlightenment, what a bullet is made of before you read the paragraph?" asked Daniel as he watched the juror's reactions to the question.

"Objection, Your Honor. Where is defense counsel going with this line of questioning?" ranted Linda as she stood up from her chair.

"Your Honor, my client, according to his statement he made to me in my office, which prosecution has a copy of, and as can be proved by defense exhibit H9, purchased a particular type of bullet. A bullet that is very unique. I am asking for the expert testimony of the ballistics technician to establish this fact."

"Fair enough, counselor. The objection by the prosecutor is noted and overruled. The witness will answer the question.

"A bullet is traditionally made of Lead, Tin and Antimony. I believe the formula is 60/20/10. If you want a harder bullet you add more Antimony and if you want a softer bullet you add more lead."

"Could you tell me if either of those bullets before you, as given to you by the San Juan County Coroner, are made of or plated with Silver?"

"Objection, Your Honor. This trial isn't about whether or not the defendant killed a werewolf or a vampire or is that what defense counsel wants us to think?" asked Linda, looking over at Daniel.

"No, my client wasn't trying to kill a werewolf or a vampire. However, Your Honor, defense exhibit H9 is a copy of a receipt from the Silverton General Store on the night of the murder. The receipt is for Silvertip® jacketed hollow point ammunition."

"Objection noted, but overruled. The witness will answer the question."

"Thank you, Your Honor."

"No, the bullets before me appear to me not to be made of nor plated in Silver."

"Thank you, Mr. Smith. Would you now read paragraph six of your report."

"The two bullets provided by the San Juan County Coroner for analysis were weighed individually on a bullet weighing scale. Bullet one weighed in at 799 grains. Bullet two weighed in at 804 grains."

"What does the weight of a bullet tell you, exactly, Mr. Smith?"

"The weight of the bullet, in grains, is then inputted into the ballistics calculator on my computer. From the weight, the ballistics calculator can tell me an approximate caliber of the weapon that the bullets may have come from. The computer can then calculate, with certain precision, the original weight of the bullets."

"What did your ballistics calculator tell you about those two bullets?" asked Daniel as he looked at the jury box.

"Your Honor, may I read the rest of the paragraph?" asked Mr. Smith.

"Proceed, as long as the prosecution doesn't have any objections?" asked Larry.

"No objections, Your Honor," said Linda, as she looked at Mr. Smith.

"Thank you, Your Honor. The ballistics calculator estimated that the bullets originally weighed 240 grains. This weight of bullet, in grains, is consistent with a .44 magnum or .41 magnum jacketed hollow point handgun round."

"I will ask you again. Is either bullet Silver?"

"No."

"Your Honor, at this time, I would like to enter into evidence as defense exhibit H9," said Daniel as he handed the copy of the receipt to Garth.

"Proceed," said Larry as he was taking some notes on the bench.

"Mr. Smith, would you please read the receipt into the court's records?" asked Daniel as he looked at Linda. She started to get up from her chair again, but sat back down for no apparent reason.

"Sure. Sold one box of .44 Smith and Wesson Special, Winchester, 200-grain, Silvertip® jacketed hollow point ammunition in a quantity of 20 rounds in the box."

"Now, I will ask you again. Are either of these two bullets, Silver?"

"No."

"I have no further questions for this witness. At this time, Your Honor, I would like defense exhibits A1 through A12 to be entered into evidence. These defense exhibits include pictures of some of the known handguns in the world that are capable of firing bullets in the .429 to .456 inch diameter range," he said.

"So noted," said Larry.

"Your witness to recross, Miss Prosecutor," said Daniel.

"I have no further questions at this time for the witness," she replied as she started seeing her case falling apart before her eyes.

Daniel sat down at his table.

"The witness is excused. The prosecution can call its next witness," said Larry.

"The People would like to call the Ironton Town Marshal to the stand," said Linda.

Jason stood up from the spectator's area and took the stand. Sergio swore him in and he sat down. Even sitting, Jason looked like he was standing. At this time, a TV/VCR was wheeled into the courtroom. Lynn set everything up and put the videotape of the crime scene into the VCR. Linda started showing photos of the crime scene and where Juan had been arrested.

"Please state for the court's record, your name and occupation," said Linda.

"I am Jason Beckman and I am currently the Ironton Town Marshal," he said.

"Thank you. Marshal Beckman, did you receive a phone call to your office or via the San Juan County Sheriff's dispatcher on December 31st of 2010 to report to the deceased's home because the caller had reported hearing gunfire?" asked Linda.

"Yes, that is correct. I have a copy of the non-emergency number tape of that conversation if it is needed, Your Honor. At the home, I found a nearly dead, young Hispanic female who had been breastfeeding her infant son when she had been shot. I immediately noticed that the couch was covered in blood. I called for an ambulance."

"What happened next?" asked Linda.

"The ambulance arrived on scene a little while later. I was inside the ambulance with the two people. The two people were taken to a local hospital where I met the attending emergency room physician.

He pronounced them both dead on arrival in my presence," said Jason, loudly, while looking at Daniel.

"Thank you, sir. Did you arrest the defendant later on that night?"

"Yes, I did."

"No further questions, Your Honor."

Daniel leaned over to Lynn and whispered something into her left ear. She started dialing the San Juan County Sheriff's Deputy's number on her cell phone. Daniel pulled a small speakerphone out of his briefcase and connected it to the cell phone. Soon, the deputy was on stand-by.

Linda waited a few minutes before looking up at Larry who called a short recess. When they had all returned, Daniel was ready for his defense. Daniel let the jury see the crime scene and the arrest scene as Jessica had filmed it. He even let the positive gunshot residue test be seen. Daniel watched the jury; they were riveted to the film being shown. Marshal Beckman took the witness stand once again.

"Marshal Beckman, didn't you find it odd that there was no blood spattering? That it appeared to have pooled into one spot on the couch?" asked Daniel.

"Objection, Your Honor. Irrelevant and immaterial to this case," said Linda.

"Your Honor, I'm about to prove relevance in that the real killer had to be standing on the deceased's property to kill them," said Daniel, looking at the jury.

"Objection overruled this time. The witness will answer the question," said Larry, looking at Jason.

"I thought it was from the cold, due to the windows being shot out by your client," replied Jason, who was starting to get nervous.

"A possibility. When you arrested my client, did you do a gunshot residue test on him?" asked Daniel as he faced the jury. They showed interest and confusion at the same time.

"No, I did not do the test," said Jason.

"Why not? Did my client confess to the shooting or what?"

"I couldn't afford the test kit but your client did confess to discharging a firearm when I initially asked him," said Jason, glaring at Daniel.

"Did you have my client in custody and interrogating him without reading him his rights?" snapped Daniel.

"No, counselor. I was merely asking your client some questions about his shooting into the hillside. He was free to go at anytime or he could have just stopped talking to me at anytime," replied Jason, furrowing his eyebrows.

"So, what you're saying is, you arrested him based upon his answers to your questions and that, allegedly, my client was free to go at anytime?"

"That's right, counselor."

"Thank you, Marshal Beckman. Did you provide ammunition for ballistics testing along with the weapon?"

"No, I did not provide any ammunition for ballistics testing because your client had used up the box of ammunition that he had on him when I was asking him questions."

"Thank you, Marshal Beckman."

Daniel picked up paperwork from the evidence table and handed it to Jason.

"Did you even bother to call the San Juan County Sheriff's Department, the Silverton Town Marshal or even the Telluride Town Marshal and ask for the test kit?"

"No, I didn't call any of those other law enforcement agencies."

Daniel showed the jury the hillside pictures.

"Marshal Beckman, would you read, to the court, the highlighted section of defense exhibit D1," said Daniel.

"Sure. The hillside is 26 feet high. Although you can see the house from where the client was arrested, no windows are present. Also, to hit the house, the shooter would have to be standing several hundred yards to the right of where the client was arrested and the shooter would have to be aiming 144 inches, or 12 feet, above the hillside to hit the house."

"Thank you, Marshal Beckman. That statement, ladies and gentlemen of the jury, came from my private investigator. One more thing, Marshal Beckman, could you read paragraph two on page four of the report to the court?"

"Sure," said Jason as he flipped through the report to the right page.

"What does that paragraph say, Marshal Beckman?"

"The bullet would have had to travel uphill at a 35 degree angle, a distance of 180-yards/60-meters, penetrate an exterior wall at that distance. The bullet fired would then have to penetrate an interior wall, into the kitchen, penetrate another interior wall on the opposite side of the kitchen. There, the bullet would have had to penetrate a small cabinet, which contained a stereo receiver. There was no damage to the stereo receiver, nor the interior/exterior walls."

"Thank you, Marshal Beckman. Is it possible for several bullets fired from a handgun to complete their journey into the bodies of the deceased?" asked Daniel as he watched the jury's reaction to his question and Marshal Beckman's answer.

"No, I do not believe such a thing is possible."

"Thank you, Marshal Beckman. Moving along now, Marshal Beckman, would you please explain to the court what we are looking at right now?" asked Daniel, showing the still shots of the positive test for gunshot residue.

"There are three green colored marks in the pictures. One on the door frame, one on the couch and one on a crooked lamp."

"Thank you, Marshal Beckman. Those marks are, in fact, a positive test for gunshot residue from the San Juan County Sheriff's Department deputy who accompanied my private investigator and myself when we toured the crime scene. She will testify to that effect, Your Honor; prosecutor."

"No need to cross-exam, Your Honor. The People will stipulate," said Linda.

"Your witness is not needed defense counsel," said Larry.

"Thank you, Your Honor. Deputy, did you hear what the judge said?"

"Yes, I did. Thank you, Your Honor, it was a pleasure," she said as she hung up the phone.

"I would like to enter into evidence defense exhibits C1 through C26."

"Objection, Your Honor. Where is defense counsel going with this?" asked Linda.

"I will wait to rule on the objection for now. Defense counsel, where are you going with the introduction of this evidence?" asked Larry.

"The introduction of this evidence proves two things, Your Honor and ladies and gentlemen of the jury," said Daniel.

"And what are those two things?" asked Linda.

"One, that the piece of bronze removed from the deceased Hispanic female's left ribcage was fired from a rifle and not a handgun. Two, the real killer, as I have said before, was, in fact, standing in the yard of the deceased," replied Daniel.

"Oh boy, Your Honor, what a fishing expedition that defense counsel has gone on," said Linda, sarcastically.

"I agree, however, defense counsel has yet to fail to prove the relevancy of any evidence introduced so far; objection overruled," said Larry, looking at Daniel.

"Thank you, Your Honor," said Daniel smiling.

"The People will stipulate, Your Honor," said Linda, exacerbated.

The court adjourned for the day after the prosecutor put a witness on the stand that stated the defendant and the deceased were intimate many times before she was killed. The prosecution, having established this fact in open court, concluded that the defendant committed a possible Crime of Passion killing when the witness stated that the deceased had broken off their relationship several months earlier. Since Daniel already knew about the relationship and he knew about the fight during his questioning of Juan, he didn't bother to cross-exam the witness.

Daniel, Lynn, Juan and Roberto arrived back at the hotel after dinner. As Daniel walked through the front doors of the hotel, the desk clerk stopped him.

"Mr. Marcos, this fax came for you a few minutes ago," he said handing Daniel the fax. Daniel motioned for Lynn to take Juan and Roberto to their room.

"Thank you," said Daniel as he took the fax and started reading it before handing the desk clerk a $50.00 bill, which the person took eagerly.

He went to his room and completely read the fax from page one to page six. He then returned to the lobby and used the lobby phone to call Marshal Beckman in the Ironton Town Marshal's office. Marshal Halverston transferred the phone call, to Marshal Beckman's cell phone.

"Yes, counselor, what can I do for you?" asked Jason.

"I just received a fax from a friend of mine who works with the FAA. He is currently in Mexico City investigating an old plane crash.

The fax states his team found some spent 7mm-08 shells and a rusty 4-round magazine that will fit a semi-automatic weapon of the same caliber."

"So what does that prove, counselor?" asked Jason as he pulled out a pen and notepad from his hotel room nightstand.

"I believe if you go out to the crime scene, you will probably find some spent, 7mm-08 shells. You might also find some footprints in the snow that may match a pair of shoes owned by Roy Georgeton."

"Anything else on this little fishing expedition, counselor?"

"Check your phone records for the night of murder. I suspect you will find the phone number that called your office to report the gunshots came from Roy Georgeton."

"That's a good one, counselor. What else can I possibly do for you?"

"I'll let you be the judge of that one, Marshal Beckman; you're a good man," said Daniel as he hung up the phone and went up to his hotel room.

"That is one crazy SOB," said Marshal Beckman as he hung up the phone in his hotel room.

As soon as Daniel entered his hotel room, his private cell phone started ringing.

"Hello?" asked Daniel.

"I found the client's parents and I managed to get them a 14-day temporary medical pass from the U.S. government for the trial. By the way, thank you for the subpoenas, they helped speed us all through customs. They identified William Georgeton from the picture I had as the one who took them to the Mexico City airport," said a very tired Jessica from the 16-hour flight back to the States.

"That's good news. Where are you now?"

"6th floor, room 619, it's a nice suite up here. I also have a bunch of receipts and I have never been more happy to be cold!"

"Get some sleep. Bring the client's parents to court tomorrow morning and make sure that they sign into the visitors register at the courthouse in case someone comes asking questions. I will expect a full report when you're able to get it to me."

"Goodnight, Daniel," she said as she tried to hang up the phone and get some sleep. Daniel interrupted her with a thought.

"Jessica, good work. Can you do me one favor before coming to court tomorrow?" asked Daniel.

"What do you want me to do?" she asked as she yawned.

"A background check on William Georgeton."

"Will do and goodnight again," she said as she hung up the phone this time and went to sleep.

The courtroom was quiet the next morning. Linda gave her closing statements and Daniel waited at the defense table before giving his closing statements. As the judge was about to instruct the jury to begin deliberations, Marshal Beckman burst into the courtroom with lots of paperwork in his right hand. Larry started banging his gavel down and yelling order in the court. Marshal Beckman whispered something into both attorneys' ears. Linda nodded her head up and down and Marshal Beckman took the witness stand.

"Your Honor, I realize that this request from defense counsel is highly irregular, but I believe the information is vital to finally clearing my client," said Daniel.

"So noted, counselor. Does the prosecution have a problem with this last minute testimony?" asked Larry.

"The People have no objections, Your Honor, pending the ballistics report from the Mesa County Sheriff's Department's crime lab," said Linda.

"Proceed, defense counsel," said Larry as he started writing things down.

"Marshal Beckman, would you please tell the court what has happened in the last 18 hours?" said Daniel as he faced the jury.

"Last night, Your Honor and the court, defense counsel called me about a fax he had received from a friend of his, whom, I found out, really does work for the Federal Aviation Administration right here in Grand Junction."

"Go on, Marshal Beckman," said Daniel.

"Defense counsel advised me to commence a search of the crime scene once again and to look for certain pieces of evidence. Marshal Halverston did find the evidence, Your Honor and the court, that defense counsel said might be found," said Jason.

"What were those pieces of evidence that Marshal Halverston found?" asked Daniel.

"Marshal Halverston found two spent shell casings from a semi-automatic rifle. The shell casings were 7mm-08 caliber and were found in the gutter above the bedroom, which is to the right of the main entrance to the house. Marshal Halverston also found and photographed faded multiple footprints."

"What happened next?" asked Daniel as he watched the jury. They were listening intently; being totally drawn into the testimony being given by Marshal Beckman.

"Marshal Halverston followed those faded footprints out of the deceased's yard, up the county road, on the left shoulder, north bound and up to the entrance gate to Roy Georgeton's property. I also did as you suggested and had the Silverton Town Marshal obtain my office phone records for the timeframe of the murder."

"What number appeared?" asked Daniel.

"Roy Georgeton's unlisted/unpublished phone number of 970-484-9797. Marshal Halverston, at my direction, obtained several more search and seizure warrants and attempted to serve them on Roy Georgeton."

"Please continue, Marshal Beckman," said Daniel as doors at the back of the courtroom opened and Juan's parents came into the courtroom.

They took seats in the very back with Jessica. Jessica walked up to Daniel and handed him a background report on William Georgeton. She then returned to the back of the courtroom. Juan's parents were looking at Daniel and smiling.

"Marshal Halverston, in the attempt to serve the search and seizure warrants got into a shootout with Mr. Georgeton. She was flown by air ambulance to the local hospital here last night; I don't know her condition as of yet."

"My sincere sympathy, Marshal Beckman," said Daniel.

"Thank you, counselor. I stayed in contact, via telephone because of time constraints of the court here, with the two San Juan County Sheriff's deputies, the Silverton Town Marshal and a Colorado Highway Patrolman who all searched Mr. Georgeton's residence after the shootout."

"What happened to Mr. Georgeton?"

"Mr. Georgeton was pronounced dead at the scene by a doctor who lives down the road from the scene and who heard the shots being fired. He tentatively listed the cause of death as multiple bullet wounds inflicted by Marshal Halverston's service weapon."

"That's too bad," commented Linda, sarcastically.

"What other evidence did the search find at the residence?" asked Daniel.

"Knowing how thorough the defense counsel would want law enforcement personnel to be, the search yielded a partially used box of 7mm-08, Bronze Point® Core-Lokt® bullets of 140 grains in weight according to what was printed on the box. There was an unopened box of the same ammunition next to that one in the gun locker that was searched."

"Was anything else found of interest?" asked Linda.

"Yes, Miss Prosecutor. A pair of shoes was discovered in the bedroom closet that were found to be a 90% match to the tread and style as the photos taken by Marshal Halverston. Also, 7 rifles, 4 shotguns, 12 handguns and ammunition for all of those weapons were also found during the search."

"That's interesting, Marshal Beckman. But, how did you know about the footprints matching the shoes?" asked Linda.

"The pictures and the shoes were flown up here with Marshal Halverston and delivered, along with one of the rifles found matching the 7mm-08 caliber and the spent shell casings. These items were all delivered to the Mesa County Sheriff's Department's crime lab for testing."

"Anything else, Marshal Beckman?" asked Daniel this time.

"Yes. The rifle seized was a semi-automatic, Remington, Model R-25 with a 4-round magazine that appeared to be fairly new. On a hunch from the information that may have been contained in the fax that the defense counsel received and at my request, the spent shell casings and the rusty magazine were sent, via overnight courier from Mexico City, to here for analysis. I am currently awaiting the crime lab results," said Jason.

"Where are the results to be delivered, Marshal Beckman?" asked Larry.

"I told the sheriff's department to deliver the results to this courtroom, Your Honor."

"Marshal Beckman, did you find a revolver at the residence?" asked Daniel.

"Yes. The Silverton Town Marshal seized a .454 Casull which is capable of firing the .44 magnum round."

"Thank you, Marshal Beckman."

"Your Honor, pending the results of the crime lab tests, I would like to request a dismissal of the charges against the defendant," said Linda.

"It's too late, Linda. Defense counsel, what do you say?" asked Larry.

"I concur, Your Honor on the dismissal of the charges. However, I also understand that it is too late," said Daniel, sitting back down in his chair at the table.

"So noted. The court will be in recess until the results are available from the crime lab," said Larry, banging his gavel down.

Daniel now had the chance to read the background report on William Georgeton. He had no military training, but he was a 14-year champion trap shooter from the State of Utah from 1994 to 2008. He could hit anywhere from 295 to 298 clay pigeons out of 300 every time. Daniel set the report down on the desktop and continued staring at the clock behind the judge's bench.

Finally at 2:00 pm, the crime lab results were made available. The judge ordered everyone back to the courtroom. The jury took their seats and the sheriff's deputy took the witness stand. Everyone in the courtroom began to hold their breath. The bailiff, Sergio, swore in the crime lab technician as she prepared to read the court the results.

"Your Honor and the court. Here are the results of the testing that was done on the rifle and associated parts that were sent to this crime lab for analysis," she started saying.

"Go ahead with the results," said Larry.

"Thank you, Your Honor. The rifle is a Remington, Model R-25. It is semi-automatic and chambered to fire the 7mm-08 caliber round. The serial number is R214761. The rusted spent shell casings and the rusted 4-round magazine submitted for testing shows that the rifle, the rusted spent shell casings and the rusted magazine submitted for testing all match 100% according to the computer," she said.

"How do you know that?" asked Linda, suspiciously.

"The extractor marks on the spent rounds match 100% to the test-fired rounds at the lab. The rounds used were some test rounds sent to us from the place they were seized by the Colorado Highway

Patrol. The submitted, 4-round, rusted magazine fits the rifle. The scratch marks are identical to those on the rusted magazine and on the inside of the magazine well. These scratch marks are identical, as well, to the spare magazine that was inside the rifle when it arrived at the lab for testing."

"Your Honor, the defense rests," said Daniel, seated at the table.

"Your Honor, the prosecution rests as well. The People move that the jury deliberate at this time," said Linda.

"So noted," said Larry.

The jury left the courtroom to deliberate as the witness left the courtroom. The jury only needed ten minutes to deliberate. When they returned to the courtroom, the jury foreman, one of the Native Americans, handed Sergio the verdict. Sergio handed the verdict to the judge. The judge read the verdict and put the piece of paper down on his bench.

"Will the defendant please rise," said Larry, picking up the piece of paper.

Daniel stood up with Juan.

"We, the jury, find the defendant, Juan Rivera, not guilty of the two counts of First Degree Murder. We, the jury, find the defendant, Juan Rivera, not guilty on two counts of Second Degree Murder," said Larry.

"Thank you, Your Honor," said Daniel.

Daniel walked over to the jury box.

"Thank you, ladies and gentlemen of the jury. I am sorry that you had to sit through all of this for nothing," said Daniel.

"The defendant is exonerated of the charges against him and is hereby released with the court's blessings," said Larry, banging down his gavel.

Daniel returned to his table where Linda cornered him.

"How did you know about Mr. Georgeton using his .454 Casull?" she asked.

"I will guess that Mr. Georgeton probably had contacts in various law enforcement agencies. These agencies probably included the Bureau of Alcohol, Firearms, Tobacco and Explosives. They were all keeping tabs on the survivors of that airplane crash. When Juan purchased his .44 magnum revolver, which he will get back, right?"

"Yes, Juan will get back all of his personal effects including his passport. But, why keep tabs on the survivors of that plane crash?" asked Linda.

"Well, I'm glad that my client will be getting his personal property back. Simple, if you kill 230 people and their children, there are that many less persons coming across the border illegally."

"I still don't understand. How did Roy know about Juan's pistol?"

"Simple, when Juan filled out the BATFE's Form 4373A, the BAFTE contact called Roy and that's when Juan was framed for the murders."

"Very good, counselor," said Linda as she left the courtroom while her legal assistant was packing up the evidence.

"There are some people who want to talk to you in the back of the courtroom and I will give you back your money," said Daniel.

"Thank you, sir. But, why give me back my money?" asked Juan.

"Those bills that your brother gave me are worth many more times their face value. Find a good collector, get a good price for them and use that money to start your life over again. Besides, I have a money back guarantee for my clients."

"Thank you, sir," said Juan as he shook Daniel's right hand.

Juan turned around to see his mom and dad standing there in the back of the courtroom. He rushed to embrace them. Daniel turned back around to see Mary standing there just behind him.

"You get an exclusive tonight. Dinner at The Winery, say, around 8:00 pm and don't be late," he said as he smiled at her.

"I won't."

She left the courtroom along with Juan, Juan's parents, Roberto and all the spectators for the trial.